WICKED DEAL

SHADOW GUILD THE REBEL BOOK 2

LINSEY HALL

For Jackson.

1

CARROW

Guild City

"I swear it won't bite," said Eve, my Fae friend.

I arched an eyebrow. "It's a dried demon head with giant fangs. It really looks like it might bite."

She laughed. "You owe me. I know it's gross, but I need to know where it came from."

I scowled and looked at the severed, dried head sitting on the counter in her cluttered shop. Hundreds of charms and potion bottles lined the shelves, but I only had eyes for the head. Its skin was wrinkled, and its horns protruded upward.

"Thank God the eyes have rotted out," I muttered. "I couldn't handle it if it looked at me."

Eve laughed again, and the raven who sat behind her hopped along the shelf, as if interested. Eve still claimed she couldn't see the raven, and I didn't push.

"Seriously, the world of magic is crazy," I said. "Having something like this is insane."

"Hey, it's rare. Normally, those heads disintegrate upon the death of the demon. I need to know why this one didn't."

"Yeah, yeah."

Eve sold magic potions and spells that she made using her Fae power, and I *did* owe her for the potions she'd given me last week. Anyway, I was trying to get my business up and running, and she was my first client. If I planned to sell my ability to magically read people and objects, then I needed to start now.

"You've got this, mate," Mac said, a big grin on her face.

I shot my other friend a grateful smile. Mac lived in the flat below me and could always be counted on for support. I drew in a deep breath, hovering my hand over the head. "One, two, three."

On *three*, I touched the head, doing my best to control my magic and see something specific about the disgusting thing. The power surged through me, seemingly stronger than ever.

That had to be impossible though, right?

I was new to this world, but I was pretty sure magic didn't grow stronger.

I focused on the vision.

There was a blast of light in my mind, followed by an eerie, high-pitched laugh that turned into a scream. It seared through my skull, making me wince.

I stumbled backward, shaking my hand.

"Well?" Eve asked.

"A laugh, a light." I scowled. "That was pathetic. I'm trying again."

I could feel their eyes on me as I approached the head once more. This kind of magic—and danger—wasn't unusual. Unlike me, they'd been born into the magical world and had known about it their entire lives. I was a newcomer, just trying to make my way.

The skin of the dried head was papery against my fingertips as I pressed them to the skull.

"Come on," I muttered. "See something useful."

The light flashed again, and the laughter howled, shrieking through my mind. I squeezed my eyes shut, trying to see through the bright light.

Please work.

I needed control of my power, damn it.

I saw nothing, but once again, the laughter turned into a scream.

Eve.

The scream was saying her name.

The magic faded from the air.

Shocked, I looked up. "It said your name. *Screamed* your name."

Eve paled slightly, her eyes dark. She drew an unsteady breath. "Thanks, that's helpful."

"That's it? This scary demon head screams your name, and that's it?"

She shrugged. "You need to get control of your magic, though. Your signature is off the charts."

I glared at her. "You're changing the subject."

"Well, we need to talk about it. But we *don't* need to talk about my deal. Not now."

"Fine." I knew when to stop poking.

"Eve's right." Mac waved a hand in front of her face. "It's like I'm lying in a freaking lavender field."

I winced. "I know."

All supernaturals had magical signatures—as many as five, each corresponding with one of the five senses. Powerful supernaturals had *all* of them, and, apparently, I was one of those. According to my friends, my magic smelled like lavender and tasted like oranges. Sounded like roaring wind and looked like a silver glow.

"Seriously, mate." Mac said. "Everyone in Guild City has to keep their signatures on lockdown or the Council of Guilds gets a bee in their bonnet."

"You do *not* want their bonnets disturbed." Eve met my gaze. "And your magic is..."

"Weird?" I asked.

"I was going to say different," Eve said. "There's something about it. And considering how serious the Council is about keeping us secret from the humans, they're not going to like the fact that you're just letting it all hang out there."

Damn it, this was bad. "Do you have more suppressor potion?"

"I do, and it's all yours, but I don't think it's going to work." Eve frowned apologetically. "You've taken too much already, and your system is used to it."

"You're going to have to think about joining a Guild, too," Mac said. "Like, soon."

"But which one?" Guild City was made up of various magical guilds, each representing one of the main magical species—fae, shifters, witches, and seers, among others.

"Whichever will have you, I guess." Mac shrugged.

I didn't like the idea of that, but if I wanted to stay here, I'd have to do it. Mac was a member of the Seers' Guild, and Eve belonged to the Fae Guild, though neither lived in her guild's headquarters.

"I'll figure it out," I said. "Soon."

"It had better be, or—"

The bell to Eve's shop jingled, and I turned.

The Devil of Darkvale stepped into the little shop, his lean, muscular form filling the door. I fought dueling instincts. Part of me wanted to step toward him. Part of me wanted to turn and run.

I stayed frozen.

In a moment, I took all of him in. The firelight scent of his magic blasted though the hodgepodge of aromas in Eve's shop. I *liked* the way he smelled, but I was careful not to inhale too much.

As usual, he was impeccably dressed. He looked like a spy, an unstoppable James Bond in a bespoke suit. It was damned unfair that men's dresswear was easy to move in *and* made the wearer look hot as hell.

He stood in the doorway, still as a statue. His sharp cheekbones and strong jaw could have been carved from granite, but his lips were full, the only part of him that looked soft. Even his silver eyes were hard as they surveyed us.

He was still ice, but I knew the heat underneath.

It would burn me—and not in a good way.

Where was the man who had bitten me?

I'd never quite felt anything like that before—I'd nearly lost my mind from the pleasure.

He stepped farther into the store, his movements graceful and smooth. The spell was broken. I snapped my mind away from the memory and focused on him.

The interior of Eve's store was like her—delicate and whimsical—and he stood out like a sore thumb. All raw power and strength. The glittering faerie lights that sparkled near the ceiling veered away from him.

"What can I do for you?" Eve's voice was flat. She didn't particularly like the Devil of Darkvale. He was Guild City's version of the mob, and as the owner of a small shop, she was beholden to him for protection from the overly enthusiastic government—the Council of Guilds. Not to mention the Witches' Guild. They'd have her head for selling magics like theirs if they could.

"I'm here to ask Carrow's help." His smile was small but genuine. Unexpected. "I'd like to hire her."

It was true that I was trying to set up shop as a clairvoyant—or whatever I was, I still wasn't sure—but I didn't have a storefront yet. The plan was to get started by helping Eve on the side.

"Oh, no, you don't." Mac stepped forward, looking like she was ready to throw down. "*You* are dangerous to her."

His gaze snapped to Mac. "Macbeth O'Connell... aren't *you* the mother hen."

His eyes glinted, and I raised a hand. "Don't even think of trying your mind thing on her."

I'd already warned him off using it on my friends, and I was immune to it, thank God.

"Wouldn't dream of it." His words were smooth as he turned to me. "As I said, I'd like to hire you."

I leaned against Eve's counter and raised a brow. "Oh?"

Mac shot me a glare.

I shrugged. I couldn't help it—I was interested. Yes, I knew he was dangerous. But damned if I wasn't a cat who was willing to risk one of her nine lives on him. "I just want to hear him out."

Mac stifled a groan.

The Devil's half smile grew the slightest bit, and he

was so damned sexy that I hated it. Worry twisted through me.

I had a nice life here. Back in the human world, my home had sucked monkey balls. Clashing with the Devil of Darkvale could get me kicked out of Guild City.

I shouldn't risk it.

"I have a man I'd like you to read," he said.

"For what?" Not that I could control what I saw from people.

"Motivation. He was trying to break in through my personal gate."

My brows rose, as did Eve's and Mac's. Guild City was hidden deep within London, a walled town formed in the medieval period—possibly by the immortal Devil of Darkvale himself—to hide the supernaturals in the city. The wall was punctuated by several gates, one the Devil's own personal access point, an impressive symbol of his power.

The fact that someone might have tried to break in through it...

Interesting.

I frowned. "Where is this person now?"

"Detained."

"You kidnapped him," Mac said.

"He was trying to break into my club from the outside."

I'd been to his base of operations a few times, but only briefly. It was well guarded. "That is an inefficient way to break into Guild City. Are you sure he wasn't trying to break into your club or your office?"

"It's also an inefficient way to break into my club."

"They're all inefficient." Eve's tone was dry. "Everyone knows the Shifters' Guild guards that place like it contains the holy grail."

"I like to do my part for the economy."

Mac scoffed. "The shifters sell protection services to anyone, and they've got plenty of work coming in elsewhere."

The Devil smiled. "Be that as it may"—his gaze turned to me—"Carrow, this may be a threat to the city as well as a threat to my empire. I could use your help. I'd pay you well."

"Ah—"

"Can I speak to you, Carrow?" Mac's voice was sharp.

"Um, yeah." I watched the Devil warily as I followed her to the back room of Eve's shop.

The Fae proprietor followed, turning back to point at the Devil. "I'm watching you. Don't touch anything."

The little room at the back was cluttered with Eve's most valuable potions. Mac whirled around as soon as we entered. "You are *not* seriously thinking of doing this, are you?"

"Um—" I frowned. "He's not so bad. He retrieved my books for me from my flat last week, remember?"

"That was nice, I'll give him that," Eve said. "I know how important those were to you."

They'd come from my friend Beatrix, who'd been murdered last year. They were all I had of hers, and he'd left them for me in my new flat.

"The books aren't the issue right now. You know what the Oracle said. Remember her?" Mac raised her brow. "That all-powerful seer who looks too legit to quit?"

I did remember the seer. She'd grabbed me at the Witches' Masquerade, her ghostly form flickering from old to young, and told me that the Devil and I were Cursed Mates.

"Do you really believe it, though?" I asked. "This Cursed Mates thing seems..."

"Fated Mates are real, and while I don't know anything about Cursed Mates, there's no way it's a good thing," Mac said.

"It's quite difficult to put a nice spin on the word *cursed*." Eve shot me an apologetic look.

"You're not wrong about that." I sighed and leaned back against the wall.

Eve raised a hand. "Oh, careful there!"

I straightened. "Right, right. Valuable potions."

"Dangerous potions." She pointed to the left of my head. "See the blue ones? They'll blow your head clean off."

"Oookay, then." I stepped away from the wall, vowing to be more careful from now on.

"Well?" Mac said. "You're saying no, right?"

"Yeah, yeah. I'm saying no." I wasn't sure I believed in the damned concept of Cursed Mates, even though it scared the hell out of me. But Mac and Eve were my Yodas in this new world, and I would listen to them. "Let's go."

I returned to the room to find the Devil standing still as a statue. It was eerie how he did that—almost as if he could turn to stone. Apparently, he really was immortal—at least in the sense that he wouldn't age, though he could be killed by trauma—and I couldn't help but wonder if it was a coping technique meant to deal with the misery of being alive forever.

"I hope you're going to say yes." His voice was impossibly smooth, a caress across my skin.

"No. I'm sorry. I'm busy here."

"You're frightened."

I bristled. "No, I'm smart. And I'm serious. I appreciate the offer, but I don't want to have anything to do with some random man who broke into your club." I shrugged. "I can't control what I see anyway, so maybe I couldn't help you."

"Practice would give you more control of your magic."

If I did this, we'd have to spend time together. Probably be close to each other...

It was tempting.

And the Council of Guilds was going to come after me if I didn't get a handle on my magic. Especially now that it seemed to be growing stronger in a way that I couldn't explain.

But...

"No." My words were firm. "But thank you."

He nodded. His face was expressionless. "I can't say I'm not disappointed, but you've made your wishes clear."

"You're going to come back and ask again, aren't you?" Mac demanded.

"I might."

Oh, he would. This wouldn't be the last I'd see of him.

"Thank you for your time, ladies." He turned and disappeared through the door, all grace and smoothness.

I looked at the others. "*That* was unexpected."

"Really?" Mac crossed her arms over her chest. "I've seen the way he looks at you. And honey, that man trying to get close is the *least* unexpected thing ever."

"She's right." Eve grimaced. "But you can't forget the Cursed Mates thing. That could be deadly."

I swallowed hard. She was right. I looked toward the door. "I hope I didn't piss him off. He's powerful, and I'm new in town."

"He's used to getting what he wants," Mac said. "But we've got your back."

I nodded shakily and turned to Eve's desk. "Let me take a look at that second object."

"Thanks." She walked around it to retrieve the golden chalice she'd asked me to look at.

The door to the shop jingled again, and I turned, expecting to see the Devil of Darkvale. Instead, a man and a woman in dark trousers and red jackets emblazoned with the crest of the Council of Guilds stood there. As with all supernaturals in Guild City, their magical signatures were on lockdown, but I could still get a feeling for what they were.

Shifters.

Something about them, a leonine grace or the cunning in their eyes, made me think of animals.

All guilds in the city sold something, and the shifters sold protection services and fighting forces. Which meant that these two were basically the cops of Guild City.

"Penelope. Garreth." Mac's voice was a bit cold. "What are you doing here?"

"We're here to escort Guild City's newest citizen to a meeting with the Council."

What the hell?

Had the Devil set this up? Was this retaliation for my refusal to help him?

My gaze flashed to Mac's and Eve's, and I swore I saw the same questions reflected there.

But no, the Devil had just left. Would he really have had time to arrange this?

He was powerful. He could have had them waiting

on standby. Would he really have done that? Thrown me under the bus?

You don't know him.

The thought flashed, and it was so true. We'd shared an almost-kiss that had nearly made me lose my mind and a bite that had *definitely* made me lose my mind, but I didn't know what it had meant to him.

And there was that little matter of the Cursed Mates thing.

He wasn't on my side.

I couldn't forget it.

I shoved him from my mind and looked at the two shifters. "Okay, I'm coming."

Garreth pulled something from his pocket, and I spotted two golden bangles. They looked like bracelets, but from the way Mac gasped and Eve scowled, I knew they couldn't be.

"Really?" Mac said. "Magicuffs?"

"You know the rules, Mac. She isn't in a guild, which makes her dangerous. Illegal."

"No person is illegal."

"This one is," Garret said.

"She's new in town," Eve said.

"She's been here a week," Penelope said. "More than enough time to approach the Council about joining a guild."

"They require this." Garreth held up the cuffs. "Not us. Let us do our jobs."

Mac growled, but I held up a hand. "It's fine."

This guild member stuff was *serious.* And I'd known I was supposed to join one—Mac had explained how things worked here. But I'd been nervous. I didn't have control of my magic or my magical signature, so I'd hesitated, reluctant to approach the Council on uneven footing.

Apparently, they weren't willing to wait.

Or the Devil had sped up our meeting.

Either way, I was going there now, and I was doing it in handcuffs.

2

The Devil

Disappointment flickered through me as I walked away from Eve's shop. Idly, I rubbed my chest, totally unfamiliar with the feeling. It had been centuries since I'd felt like this.

One, because I rarely wanted anything.

And two, because if I *did* want something, I got it.

And I wanted Carrow.

Not just her help, but the woman herself.

And damned if it wasn't strange.

Faint morning sunlight flickered though a large tree that grew up through one of the Fae shops. The trees were a rarity in London, but there were quite a few here in Guild City, especially around the Fae enclaves.

Sunlight sparkled through the green leaves, and I marveled that I could now see the brilliant colors. That I could now smell the freshness of the leaves and taste the dawn on the air. Feel of the cool morning breeze on my skin.

Because of Carrow.

She'd brought me back to life. Her blood, specifically. I'd drunk the blood of thousands over the years. First, in a frenzy. When I'd been made nearly five hundred years ago, I'd fallen into the blood lust that plagued all turned vampires.

Unlike most of them, I'd survived, keeping to the shadows so the vampire hunters wouldn't find me.

But I'd never drunk blood like hers. It had returned the sharp senses the turning had stolen. Back then, I'd retained my excellent hearing, but the rest...gone. I'd had new skills to compensate, but I hadn't realized how much I'd missed seeing the full spectrum of color in the world. Smelling and tasting and *feeling.*

There was something special about her—about her blood—that had done this to me. The Oracle had said she would thaw me, but I'd dismissed her.

Now, I didn't know what to believe.

I stepped up onto the pavement in front of the Fae shop, trying to force Carrow from my thoughts. The owner was out sweeping the step, and he moved away from me, pressing himself against the wall.

I nodded at him and continued walking.

I reached the corner and looked back at Eve's shop. Pathetic, perhaps, but I couldn't help it.

Two figures stepped out, both wearing the signature red and black of the Council of Guilds. Penelope and Garreth, shifters who worked on the payroll.

I'd only been gone a few minutes, and already they were coming out?

A smaller figure stepped out behind them, her brilliant gold hair shining in the light. I still couldn't believe how beautiful she was, now that I could see her fully.

The unexpected glint of gold at her wrists caught my eyes.

Magicuffs.

Protectiveness surged inside me, followed by rage.

How dare they cuff her?

I stepped toward them, a blood lust rising in my veins that I hadn't felt in hundreds of years, but the sight of her in danger...

At the last moment, I pulled myself back.

No. That wasn't the way to handle the situation.

I shoved the beast back in its cage. I'd learned over the years that the best way to power was through cunning first, strength second.

But fates, it was hard to remember that when my only desire was to kill the shifters who'd cuffed her.

Carefully, I drew in a deep breath.

I would find out what was going on and remedy it.

I would protect her.

The urge was strange, but undeniable. I embraced it.

Carrow

I'd left my friends behind in Eve's shop, telling them to stay put. Mac had resisted, but when she'd finally nodded, I'd caught a gleam in her eye. It was the same gleam she'd had when she'd let me go into the Devil's club alone—she'd said I'd need someone on the outside to break me out.

My heart hammered as I followed the guards, and I hoped I wouldn't need Mac's help. This had to be a formality, right?

All the same, I couldn't help but notice the nerve-racking similarity between this and my life a week ago, when I'd been cuffed by the human police while standing over a freshly murdered body.

I was spending way too much time in handcuffs lately.

The shifters were silent as they led me down the narrow, cobbled streets of Guild City. Tudor-style buildings rose two and three stories tall on either side, their dark wooden beams and white plaster walls like something out of a movie. There were parts of human London that had buildings like these, but none that had so many of them.

And no neighborhood on the mundane side of London had shops full of magic. Guild City reeked of the stuff, and I loved it. I tried to focus on that as they led me to Council headquarters. Focusing on the dancing magic in the windows kept me from freaking out.

I'd seen the headquarters a few times while walking with Mac or Eve through the center of town. As we approached it from a side street, the massive building loomed. It was huge and Gothic, wider than it was tall. The walls and ornate statues were covered with black soot. According to Mac, it had once been a church of all faiths—Fae, witch, shifter, demon, and all the rest—but it was now the headquarters of the Council of Guilds. Locals called it Black Church because of the exterior, and I'd never heard another name for it.

No one seemed to notice that it was a creepy sounding name for a creepy looking place.

The guards led me closer, and we crossed the large open square in front of it. There was no one about at this hour, which was odd, considering it was midmorning. It gave the whole procession an ominous feel, and as we ascended the wide stairs to the two huge doors, I shivered.

"The Council has convened to meet with you," Penelope said.

"Should I be honored?"

"No," Garreth said. "Decidedly not."

Well, shit.

They led me through the massive doors into an entryway that was done up in dark wood and marble. We passed through it quickly, entering the main part of the church. The room was enormous, the round shape so reminiscent of Temple Church that I shuddered.

Only a week before, I'd stopped a necromancer from murdering a woman in Temple Church. He'd chosen the location in the human world for a reason I still didn't understand, but it had been horrifying to witness the beginning of his ritual. The idea that such dark magic existed out there...

I shot Garreth and Penelope a look. "I thought the Council might owe me for my role in stopping the necromancer."

Garreth looked down at the cuffs. "Apparently not, if those cuffs are any indication."

Ugh. "Too true."

The round main room of Black Church was much larger than Temple Church had been, and circular benches surrounded the open space in the middle. A dozen cloaked figures watched us from the benches, their stares burning into me. They sat spaced apart, as though they didn't like one another.

I recognized a few of them right off the bat—not the people so much, but the guilds they represented. There was a woman with long dark hair topped by a pointed witch's hat. Her cloak's black velvet sparkled with the occasional diamond. She was an easy one to identify—Witches' Guild.

Near her sat a man with a black goatee and a midnight blue cloak. He looked like a wizard with questionable motives straight out of a children's book—he had to be a sorcerer.

The shifter was a man with broad shoulders, wavy dark hair, and piercing blue eyes. He was handsome, in an earthy way, and something about his energy screamed power. Raw, animal energy that could be translated quickly into killing force. From what I knew, shifters could turn into any animal, but this guy was a big predator. My money was on a tiger or a bear, or maybe even something magical, like a griffon.

The others were harder to identify, but I knew there had to be a seer, a mage, a Fae, a vampire, and quite a few others.

I kept my gaze on all of them as I walked to the center of the room, determined not to show fear. Some of them had to have inhumanly good hearing—the shifter, for sure—and I prayed they couldn't hear my frantic heartbeat.

It was hard not to wish that my friends were the

leaders of their guilds so that they could be here with me, advocating on my behalf. But they were like me, wanting to go their own way. They didn't live in the towers associated with their guilds, as many members did.

The sorcerer stood. He was handsome, albeit in a sharp and slightly scary fashion. I went through my mental index, pulling up all the info I had on sorcerers. They were known for being insanely intelligent, cunning, and loyal to their own kind. They sold big magic but didn't let you out of their sight while you used it. And they always attained their goals, no matter what. Though they were frightening, they were to be respected.

In the distance, I spotted a tiny shadow low to the ground: Cordelia, my raccoon familiar, watching from the shadows. She kept tensing and moving forward, as if she were going to dart out and try to save me.

Stay there! I tried to scream with my mind. She was no match against the Council of Guilds, and I wanted to play by their rules, anyway.

If it involved getting these cuffs off.

"Carrow Burton." The sorcerer's deep voice echoed smoothly around the chamber. "I am Ubhan, the representative of the Sorcerers' Guild."

"Hello."

"Do you know why you are here?"

I bit my lip, unsure of what to say. Maybe it was because I hadn't claimed a guild or had no control over my magic or my signature. Or maybe it was because of the powerful gem that I'd taken from the necromancer last week when we'd stopped him mid-ceremony. He'd made it from the organs of his victims, turning a heart and a liver into a crystal called Orion's Heart. I'd managed to grab it with my bare hands, which was apparently very rare.

I'd thought about turning it in to the Council for safekeeping—they'd wanted me to—but I'd decided against it. I didn't trust them. Instead, I wore it on a chain around my neck, tucked under my shirt and out of sight.

I didn't mention the gem, though part of me wished I'd given it to them. Anything to avoid this.

"Is it because I haven't chosen a guild?" That had to be the smallest crime, so I'd confess to it.

"In part," Ubhan said. "You have been in our city for a full week, yet you have not visited us to claim a guild."

I'd known it was important, but I hadn't realized it was the kind of important that would get me hauled in like a criminal.

"You also have no control of your magical signature," Ubhan said. "You are a danger to yourself and the city as long as you cannot hide your magic."

"But humans never come here." The words popped out of me, and I wished I could bite them back. Hesitantly, I added, "Isn't that why we must control our signatures? So that they don't sense what we are?"

"Precisely." Ubhan nodded. I could feel the gazes of everyone else in the room, but he was apparently their voice. "It is irrelevant if humans come here. If we don't control our signatures, Guild City is at risk. It is hidden within London by powerful magic, but only because we control our signatures. If we lose control of them, the shield spell weakens. Everyone in Guild City controls their signatures, and you should be no exception."

"Of course not." I shook my head. "I'll practice more, I promise."

"You will also join a guild."

"Which one?" I was sort of like a seer because I could read information from people and objects. But I was a little bit like a mage, too, according to Mac. And there were psychic witches who could do things a bit like I could. My skills were somewhere in the middle of the guilds.

The leader of the Witches' Guild leaned forward. "We'll take her." She looked at me. "I am Cartimandua."

I smiled gratefully at her and inclined my head. I'd been to a party at the Witches' Guild. It was like a crazy sorority house full of magic. It would be fun, no doubt, but I still bristled at the idea. I didn't want to be forced into joining some group. I had a nice life already in the making with my new flat and Mac and Eve and Quinn.

"No," Ubhan said. "Her magic is different, strange. She needs to be tested."

Several others in the room nodded in agreement, and a chill went over me.

"A test?" I hated that my voice sounded squeaky.

Was this, like, a magic test? There was no way I could pass a test.

"It is simple." The sorcerer gestured to the middle of the room. "Approach the star on the ground and stand upon it."

My gaze followed his gesture, and I spotted a metal seven-pointed star laid into the middle of the stone floor. It was at least four meters across and gleamed a dull bronze.

"What will happen when I do?" I could hear the skepticism in my voice.

"Magic will link you to whichever guild you are meant to join." Ubhan flicked his hand, clearly wanting me to just get on with it.

I strode toward the metal star, ready to run if things got weird. *Where* I would run was another thing entirely, since I couldn't hide from them in Guild City, and I was unwilling to leave. But I'd be ready to move if I had to.

I stopped in the middle of the star, feeling the eyes of the entire Council on me. A low chant began, coming from somewhere else in the church, raising the hair on the back of my neck.

The words were indistinguishable, but magic pulsed

in the air. It pressed in on me, heavy as a curse. A noise from above caused a hush of expectation to fill the room. I looked upward as a star-shaped mark at the top of the domed ceiling twisted and opened, sending a shaft of light down upon me.

It slammed into me, throwing me to the ground. Pain and panic flared just before I blacked out.

3

Carrow

Agony seared my skull, and I blinked blearily, trying to clear my vision.

Why was I lying on the floor?

The cold stone was hard beneath me as I tried to sit up gracefully.

Failure.

I wobbled upright and took in the room around me.

A dozen figures stared down at me from their perches on the benches that surrounded the circular room with the soaring ceiling.

Black Church.

Of course.

I staggered upright, pain still throbbing in my head.

The stone beneath me was the bronze star—that's why it had been so cold. The light that had knocked me out had faded, and the star-shaped hole in the ceiling above me had closed.

There was the distinct feeling of shock in the air, and the faces of those around me were slack.

"What happened?" I demanded. "How long was I out?"

Which guild had chosen me? And holy crap, was that their idea of a test? It had been brutal and stupid. What good was knocking me out?

The sorcerer flicked his hand at the two guards who had brought me here, Garreth and Penelope. They jerked to attention and strode toward me. Garreth reached for his pocket again, and I tensed. When he pulled out cuffs, I nearly hissed.

"You're not putting those on me." I stepped back.

"Ubhan insists." His voice wasn't even apologetic.

My heartbeat raced in my head. "What are you doing?"

"You are not suited for any guild." The sorcerer's voice boomed out over the empty room. "Your magic has been rejected by Guild City."

Rejected?

"No. That can't be possible." I had no idea what was even possible here, but I wasn't going to leave Guild City. This was my new home, the only place where I fit in.

"This is the way." The sorcerer glowered. "You'll be

put in a holding cell until we decide what to do with you."

"No, that's—" I began, but my lips glued themselves together, as if by magic. I tried to force them open, to protest, but they wouldn't budge.

Damn. It *was* magic.

Wildly, I glared around the room at whoever had done it. Shifty eyes moved so as not to meet mine.

Hang on....

Were they *afraid* of me?

No way. They were all insanely powerful supernaturals, the leaders of their guilds. There was no way they were afraid of me.

Not possible.

Garreth stepped toward me, and I tried to dodge. My feet slowed like I'd plunged them into syrup. I strained against the magic, my muscles burning as I tried to break away. Garreth grabbed me easily and snapped the cuffs on. Penelope came to my other side and gripped my arm.

They began to drag me from the room, and though I tried in vain to struggle, I was barely able to move. My shout was muffled behind a magical gag, building up in my throat as frustration and fear welled within me.

Cordelia hid in the corner, trembling as her eyes glinted with rage and cunning.

As we passed one of the benches on our way to the

door, I caught a snippet of conversation from two supernaturals whose species I didn't recognize. A man and a woman, both slight and mean-looking.

"Never seen anything like it," the woman said.

The man nodded. "She'll have to stay locked up, there's no question."

"Not even evicted?"

"With power like hers? Can't be allowed to roam free."

I caught the gaze of the man who'd spoken, seeing into beady black eyes that gleamed with a dark satisfaction.

He'd deliberately spoken loudly enough for me to hear, that bastard.

He was talking about leaving me locked up forever because my magic was weird, a kind they did not understand and feared.

Anxiety thrashed inside my chest like a living beast. I struggled against the guards' strong grip as they dragged me toward the door.

But as we passed through, another figure appeared.

The Devil of Darkvale.

He looked impeccable—though angry—as he walked toward the main meeting room.

"Your fault!" I tried to shout through the gag. It came out muffled and ineffective, and I wanted to kick him.

I almost did, too. The only thing that stopped me

was the fact that I probably wouldn't land a good one and would just look like an ass.

He'd sicced the Council on me when I hadn't helped him with his damned intruder. What a bastard. I was going to get him for this. If I didn't have the magic to do it, I would grow it.

Hell, I would burn down his whole damned world for this.

The guards dragged me through the church, heading toward the back and down a set of stone stairs. We descended deep into the earth, the walls around us glinting with dampness and furred with dark moss. A corridor revealed eight cells below the church. They appeared ancient, tiny rooms of stone with metal bars. The whole place had the feeling of an underground world, as if there were more to Guild City below the surface.

The guards put me in the cell, and the only thing I could be grateful for was the fact that they didn't shove me. That didn't stop them from slamming the gate in my face, though.

I stared out through the bars, swallowing hard against the fear.

How would I get out of this?

The Devil

I strode past Carrow as she was led away in magicuffs. Hot anger surged inside me, turning my blood molten. I wanted to stop, to jerk the cuffs off her and knock out both guards.

Instead, I looked away from her.

It made something feel strange in my chest—unpleasant—but I couldn't reveal weakness to the Council. And *she* was a weakness.

I'd been delayed in getting there by my attempt to discover the Council's intentions. As much as I'd wanted to run after her outside of Eve's shop, I'd resisted. Information was power, and I always came prepared. As much as I wanted to tear Black Church apart and put these bastards in their place, it would never work. I couldn't outright murder people anymore.

Not often, at least.

I drew in a breath as I entered the main meeting room of the Council of Guilds, trying to calm myself. The heavy weight of ceremony imbued the air. As usual, it annoyed me.

I scanned the room, taking in the crowd, and felt my eyebrows rise. Every guild representative was here. Carrow had merited a big crowd. My gaze lingered on the Vampire Guild's leader. Mateo and I had an arrangement, and it worked. Primarily because I kept strict control of it.

There wasn't a chance in heaven or hell that I'd participate in a guild, but even I wasn't exempt from the Council's demands, so I did what I did best.

I bought my way in.

Thus, the Vampire Guild claimed me as theirs, and I didn't cause any problems for them. I certainly didn't go to guild meetings.

Mateo gave me a brief nod, his pale hair gleaming in the light. Unlike me, he had been born a vampire and therefor was not immortal. Youth gleamed in his eyes despite the fact that he was somewhere in his sixties.

Everyone's eyes looked young when you were immortal.

Mateo stood and inclined his head. "Devil. We were not expecting you."

"I imagine not." I stopped near Mateo, avoiding the star in the middle. Powerful magic resonated around that star, and I wanted nothing to do with it. "I see you've met our new resident."

There was a chorus of yeses and nods from the gathering. I could feel the expectation on the air—the anxiety—as they waited to see what I would do. I had control of this Council in a very complicated way. Each person here did my bidding because I bribed them, threatened them, or compelled them with my powers.

It was never an easy process, however. I didn't want to be a ruler—too much responsibility. This suited me better, but it could be complicated.

My power wasn't absolute, of course. It was all a careful balance. I wouldn't be able to free Carrow forever, but I would be able to get her out today.

Then we'd deal with the rest.

I pinned each with a gaze. "What do you want with the girl?"

"She has powerful magic that must be controlled." Ubhan's eyes flickered with dislike.

"Are you sure you don't just want Orion's Heart?" Her ability to hold that gem was proof enough of her powerful magic. But some members of this Council—the Sorcerers' Guild, particularly—coveted such items.

"It's a powerful talisman," the sorcerer said. "It shouldn't be held by one with such poor control of her magic."

His logic was sound, but Carrow was different. Immune from the rules, as far as I was concerned.

"She failed the guild selection ceremony." There was triumph in Ubhan's voice.

"What do you mean, *failed*?" It was an ancient spell meant to determine what species a supernatural was. "It can't fail."

"It did."

That was strange. And it would have to be dealt

with. Even I understood the importance of belonging to a guild. The city had been founded on that principle.

"Be that as it may, she stopped a necromancer. She is new to our city, but she could be a very valuable asset."

My voice stung like a whip. "She is *not* valuable if she is locked up in the dungeons below."

There was a grumbling from the two who always fought me the hardest: Ubhan, the sorcerer, and Nyla, the elemental mage. I narrowed my gaze on them, using my magic silently. There were those in this room who suspected that I could compel without using my voice, but they'd never worked up the courage to question me about it.

I let my magic reach out to them, floating silently and invisibly on the air to seep into their minds and make them amenable to my goals. I used this gift rarely —better to let people think I controlled others with my voice.

"Carrow failed the guild ceremony because she has not mastered her magic yet." I was almost positive that wasn't the case, but I imbued my voice with such certainty and power that they'd be forced to agree with me. For now. "I will take her as my responsibility and teach her to control her magic. I guarantee she will be a safe member of the community. And when her training is complete, she will find a guild."

There was more grumbling from Ubhan, but his eyes were blurring just slightly, indicating that my magic was working on him. I knew to look for that sign, but hopefully, the others did not.

"Her gift is a simple one, albeit powerful," I said. "She can do no harm by touching things or people and reading information from them."

She could do a hell of a lot of harm, in fact, if there was anyone on this Council involved in shady dealings and she touched one of their possessions. She was in the business of secrets, though I doubted she saw it that way.

"That's hardly all she can do," protested Nyla.

"Do you have something to hide?"

"I am honest and above reproach."

She was laying it on a bit thick, but I merely inclined my head, imbuing my voice with suggestive power. "I will take her under my protection and ensure that she is no threat to us."

There was less blustering this time, and I could tell that my magic was working on them.

Ubhan stood and gazed around the assembly, garnering a nod from each one present before he looked at me. "We will release her on the condition that she learns to master her magic and proves she is no threat. But hear me well, Devil. If she cannot do it to *my* satisfaction, she goes back to the dungeons."

I disliked the emphasis on *my*—he had an agenda here, no question—but I merely nodded and stored the information away for later. I'd spent so much of my early life on bloody rampages. I infinitely preferred manipulation and diplomacy.

"You've made a wise decision." I turned and strode out, not bothering with farewells.

I heard a few annoyed huffs behind me, but my thoughts were already on Carrow. She'd spent at least ten minutes in the dank cells. I didn't want her to spend a second longer down there.

Penelope, the shifter guard, followed me as I moved quickly toward the stairs and into the dungeons. This place was archaic, but it did have its uses.

Imprisoning Carrow should not be one of them.

I caught sight of her standing at the bars of her cell, her golden hair gleaming in the dim light. I blinked, unable to believe how beautiful she looked—how bright and luminous. She'd brought my senses back to life, according to the Oracle, and I wanted to know more. I'd long ago heard the prophecy that someone would thaw me, and it seemed that was true.

"You did this." She glared at me, spitting fire with her eyes.

A raccoon sat at her side, glaring at me.

"I did not." I clenched my fists, wanting to tear the bars off their hinges and slam them into Ubhan's smug face. How *dare* he do this to her?

"Unlock the cell." My voice gritted with anger, and Penelope hurried to comply.

Carrow looked from the guard to me, confusion on

her face. I caught the briefest whiff of her lavender magic and the scent of her skin—something undefinable that made me want to bury my face in her neck and—

I wanted to bite her.

No.

I would not think of that. Not here, no matter how tempting the idea. Now that I'd had a taste of her—my first in centuries directly from another person—I wanted more.

The heavy metal lock *snick*ed as Penelope turned the key. The door swung open, and Carrow and the raccoon darted out. She was close enough to touch, and I almost reached for her.

But no.

I'd done terrible things in my life. I didn't deserve to touch her. Nor did I have permission. Again, I clenched my fists.

"You orchestrated this somehow," she said. "Got me locked up because I wouldn't help you, and now you're conveniently here to rescue me. That is right up your alley."

I opened my mouth to deny it, but... "You're right. It's something I'm capable of." The fact that I'd manipulated and threatened the entire Council to get her out of here proved that my morals were nonexistent. "But in this case, I did not. It is coincidence."

She scoffed and crossed her arms.

Penelope shifted uncomfortably, and I cut her a quick look. "You may go."

The guard scurried away, almost running up the stairs.

"It's true," I said. "This is coincidence. Think of Ubhan. Do you truly think he doesn't want you here, locked up for his own reasons? He wants to force you to use your magic to help him."

"Why not hire me?" There was the slightest trace of doubt in her voice. "I'm starting a business selling my services."

"He could. Unless he wants you to read something. Unless he's worried you will reveal terrible information about him or his allies. Not to mention your power."

Her eyes flickered.

"The spell that would assign you to a guild couldn't work on you. Your magic is too strong, too strange."

Her jaw tightened. "You're here now. Why?"

"Because I'm fond of you." *Fond* was such a weak word. It felt awkward on my tongue, but I didn't know what else to say that wouldn't scare the hell out of her.

"Fond? That's a ridiculous word."

We agreed on something, it seemed. "You're right. Frankly, I don't know how I feel about you. But I do want you." I could be honest about that. I *had* to be honest about that. I wanted her more than I wanted her blood, more than I wanted anything.

"You want my magic."

"That as well."

"I don't know how to process this."

"Why don't you start by following me out of here?"

She drew in an unsteady breath and nodded. "Hell, yes. Let's go."

4

CARROW

I followed the Devil out of the horrible old church, moving at a quick pace alongside him. I didn't want to spend a second more in that hellish place. Cordelia followed silently at my heels.

My mind spun as we walked through the damp, dark hallways.

He wanted me.

Not just my power.

Me.

I couldn't deny it. I could feel it coming off him like a heady scent that spun my mind and caressed my skin. I'd felt it during our near kiss, and I'd *definitely* felt it when he'd bitten me. That bite had been better than any sex I'd ever had.

To be fair, it had all been mediocre sex, but still.

I shot him a surreptitious glance, taking in his lean, powerful grace. He was the most beautiful man I'd ever seen, but also the most terrifying. Not just for his magic, but for his physical power as well.

His strength and speed, not to mention his charm, were enough to get him whatever he wanted in life. Add his mind control powers to it, and no one could mount a defense against him.

Except me.

His powers didn't work on me.

He was stronger than me, but my mind was my own.

Except for the fact that I wanted him right back, but it would do me no good if I gave in to those damned instincts.

Cursed Mate.

Especially given that little prophecy that I didn't understand. Did he know about it?

We approached the main exit, and the sight of the two figures by the door drew my mind from the Devil.

The guards watched us as we left, and I barely resisted hissing at them. Garreth and Penelope. Their names were going on my list of people to avoid.

The afternoon sun welcomed us as we walked out onto the massive front steps of the church. The square spread before of us, its pale stone gleaming. Cordelia disappeared immediately, and I couldn't blame her.

Mac, who'd clearly been waiting outside, launched herself at me. "You're out!"

She threw her arms around me and squeezed tight. I hugged her back. "You've been hanging around out here?"

"Of course." She pulled back and looked at me like I was crazy. "I'd have been in there, too, if Tweedle Dee and Tweedle Dum hadn't kept me out."

I grinned. "Thanks, Mac."

"Duh, I've got your back." She grabbed my arm, obviously ignoring the Devil. "Come on, we're getting out of here."

"Not quite yet." The Devil's voice was quiet but commanding. It wrapped around me and squeezed, like an overly tight hug that I both liked and loathed.

I turned back to him. "Is it time to pay the piper?"

"If I am the piper, then yes."

"Seriously?" Mac glowered at him. "Can't you just do something out of the goodness of your heart for once?"

"Perhaps. If I had a heart." His slate-gray eyes were so cold that I believed him when he said it.

Yet I'd felt the heat in him, so deeply buried beneath the ice.

There was a heart in there, albeit one that no longer worked. Sure, it pumped blood—vampires weren't undead like I'd believed when I'd known nothing about this world—but his heart was probably as shriveled as he seemed to imagine.

Almost.

Mac crossed her arms over her chest. "What do you want, O Heartless One?"

"Carrow's help with the issue that I requested earlier."

My mind raced. "Will you let me go if I don't help you?"

"No."

Still, he might let me go. I knew he wasn't a total bastard. There'd been a *connection* when he'd bitten me.

But I had a big problem with the Council, and it seemed to all stem from my lack of control over my magic. I *had* to learn how to control it. I could feel it inside me, growing.

Mac and Eve had tried to help, even Quinn. But they hadn't understood it any better than I had. The tricks they used to control their signatures didn't work for me.

But the Devil...

He was powerful. And old. He would know all the tricks.

"Help me learn to control my magic," I said. "I don't know how you got me out of there, but I can't imagine it's permanent. You're right. They want me for something, and I need to learn how to hide my magic. I don't want them to give them *anything*."

"You're very clever," he said.

"Of course I am."

A grin tugged at the corner of his mouth. "As it happens, that is one of the conditions of your release. You must learn to control your magic—not only so you follow the rules of Guild City, but so you might join a guild." He inclined his head to the side. "And from a more practical standpoint, you don't want them to know how powerful you are."

"You'll help me?"

"Indeed. You're under my protection, as it were."

"Control, you mean."

He shrugged. "Semantics."

"Control. You got me out, and you can convince them to throw me back in."

"Not if you become proficient enough in magic that you enter a guild. Then you'll be a law-abiding citizen, and they can't touch you."

"That won't stop them from trying," Mac said.

"Perhaps. But they'll have less of a leg to stand on."

Mac looked at me and the Devil, her expression calculating. "I want you to promise you'll have her back with the Council even after all of this is over."

"Done." He spoke the words so quickly that it surprised me.

"Good." Mac appeared pleased.

The Devil looked at me. "I will train you."

A shiver of heat ran through me, an icy-hot sensation that made my nerve endings light up. The idea of being *trained* by the Devil of Darkvale made my heartrate skyrocket.

I nodded. "Good. And I'll help you with the guy who broke in through your gate."

"It's a deal."

A wicked deal.

"Let's get it over with, then." I looked at Mac. "I'll see you at home."

She nodded, then glared at the Devil. "You be careful. I'm watching you."

"Of course."

I hugged Mac quickly. "Thanks again for coming to get me."

"Yeah. 'Course."

I said goodbye and followed the Devil through the streets, every cell of me aware of him. We were at odds, yet somehow, that made the attraction more intense.

"You really don't know why this guy tried to break into your club?" I asked.

"No idea."

"And he's waiting there for us."

"Yes. Waiting."

His tone on the last word was weird. "Oh crap, he's dead, isn't he? That's why you can't question him, and you need me."

He shot me a look that I could almost describe as apologetic. "He died upon passing through the gate. It's a spell that takes out anyone who uses it that shouldn't."

"That's terrible!"

"He was warned. You can feel the magic as you pass though."

"He must have been desperate."

"He had a charm breaker on him that he thought would work. He was too cocky. He entered my club for a reason, and I want to know what it is."

"Fine. I'll touch the body." I shivered at the idea of it. I disliked touching dead things, full stop, but there was something deeper and darker at work here. I could feel it. "I'll help you with this, and then you'll help me practice my magic. I'm going to get good, and I'm going to do it quickly."

"I believe it."

We'd arrived at the tall stone tower that contained his club. The façade was dark and intimidating, and I knew the interior to be no better. It suited him perfectly.

The two shifter bouncers inclined their heads and opened the doors.

I nodded at them, then muttered. "They're much better than Penelope and Garreth."

"My guards will never lock you up."

"Hmm. Not sure if I believe that."

In the small entranceway, he turned to me. "I am serious. You are safe here."

The intensity in his voice made me shiver.

Cursed Mates.

If he was determined to protect me—because he

was, I could feel it—then why were we Cursed Mates? Where did the "cursed" come in?

I needed to learn a hell of a lot more about this. And eventually ask him.

Not now, though.

Miranda, the hostess who stood behind the podium, beamed at us. She wore the same black-pencil-skirt-and-blouse uniform as usual, looking perfectly pressed and deadly.

The Devil stopped briefly in front of her. "How are things?"

"Going smoothly as usual. The body is waiting for you." Her gaze flicked to me, calculating. "I hope you're right about her."

Irritation blazed, followed by the slightest prick of jealously. There was more between these two than just club owner and hostess.

But I should *not* be jealous.

That was nuts.

"Thank you, Miranda."

The Devil and I departed, and as we entered one of the many dark, labyrinthine hallways, I leaned toward him. "She's not just the hostess, is she?"

"She's my second in command. A banshee. Smart and deadly."

I grinned, begrudgingly liking the idea of this Miranda. I never held on to jealousy long, and I liked the idea of a banshee second. Honestly, I liked this whole new world. It scared the crap out of me sometimes, but it was impossible not to think about how cool it was.

A frisson began to prickle at my skin as we approached a door at the end of the hall. We'd avoided the club entirely, and we were nearly to the body.

"We don't have to stay long," the Devil said, sounding a bit uncomfortable.

"What's wrong with you?"

He hesitated, his brow creasing. "I…find myself uncomfortable making you do this."

My eyebrows shot all the way to my hairline. "What?"

He just shrugged.

"Huh." Surprising. He was so ruthless and efficient. The fact that he was feeling guilty about twisting my arm was… "That's unexpected."

"I could not agree more. Come." The iceman had returned, ruthlessly dragged to the surface, it seemed. He turned and opened the door.

I followed him into the small room. There was a table in the middle, and on it was a body. It appeared to be completely uninjured, though it reeked of dead fish.

I held my nose. "What the heck is that?"

"That is dark magic."

"Whew, it's foul." Mac had explained to me that dark magic had terrible signatures—it reeked, sounded awful, and felt even worse. But this was more than I'd imagined.

"It makes it easy to determine those with ill intent, at the very least."

"And he didn't control his signature like you do?"

"Not as well, no. Guild City is fairly unique in that. It's part of our culture—our laws—to require all supernaturals to keep careful control of their signatures. Only powerful supernaturals can do that, which requires everyone in the city to work hard at it. The rest of the world doesn't care as much."

"Humans don't notice that supernaturals have magical signatures?"

"No. Their senses are less attuned to it, and when they do pick up on it, they blame it on something else."

"Yet Guild City is fanatic about it."

"It's been that way for hundreds of years. It helps us hide better. We're one of the few cities of our kind—enormous yet hidden within an even larger human settlement. We need to be more careful than, say, Magic's Bend in America because our shield spell is different than theirs. That city is located far from human settlements and can be more lenient with the rules."

"I think I might like it better there."

"Plenty of people do."

I'd been joking, mostly. I couldn't imagine any place better than Guild City. But we were standing over a corpse that reeked of fish, and maybe Magic's Bend had fewer of those.

I turned to the body and inspected it. The guy's dark magic was so pungent and obvious that I felt a little bit less bad about his death. He didn't necessarily look like a jerk, but I had a feeling that if he'd been alive and I'd been able to look into his eyes, I wouldn't have liked what I saw there.

Shaking slightly, not certain I wanted to see what he would reveal to me, I pressed my fingertips to his cold arm.

The world detonated around me, a vision blasting into my head.

Black Church exploding in a fireball of blue magic. The streets around it going up in flames of green and orange. Shouts and screams, magic flying through the air. The gates collapsing, and London—*human* London—looking in on Guild City and seeing all our secrets.

I gasped, stumbling backward.

The Devil broke my fall. His hands were gentle on my arms as he steadied me. "What is it? Are you all right?"

I tried to catch my breath, the vision still flickering in my mind. "Guild City is under attack. It's going to blow up."

5

The Devil

"Blow up?" I asked. "As in, the city will explode?"

Carrow's face had turned entirely white, and it appeared to cost her an effort to nod. "I saw it."

"When?"

"I'm—I'm not sure." She looked at the body, apprehension in her gaze. "I'm going to try to look again."

She raised a hand toward the corpse, trembling slightly.

Something tugged in me at the sight. I didn't like it. I didn't want her to do anything she was uncomfortable with.

Bloody hell, I hadn't felt anything like that in forever. Not *ever*.

I barely resisted rubbing my chest, as if I could drive the feeling out.

It didn't matter, anyway. If Guild City was going to blow up, we needed to know when.

She touched the body and jerked, then closed her eyes. "Three days' time."

"Only three days." Was the date significant? "Who is he?" I had an idea of who he worked for, but not who *he* was specifically.

"No idea. I can't get any more information."

"Why not?"

"Chill, okay?" Her gaze snapped to me. "I'm doing my best."

"I apologize." I'd said those words many times over the centuries. I'd never really meant them until now. Guilt streaked through me at pressing her. I needed to try to be more careful.

She was a...person to me.

Until now, everyone in my life had been a pawn. No more alive than a chess piece.

But not her.

And I'd had no practice at dealing with people.

I'd need to be a fast learner.

She frowned. "My magic gets tapped out. It's like fatigue. Like, you can only run so much until you pass out."

"That's normal. All magic needs to be recouped.

Strong supernaturals have the ability to store more magic to use, but even they run out."

"Can practice make me stronger?"

"It can make you more skilled with the magic you have, but it can't make you more powerful in the sense that you can't expand the reservoir of magic inside you."

"Oh."

"I wouldn't worry about it too much. You're already incredibly powerful. I can feel it."

"You can feel it because I can't keep it on lockdown."

"Precisely."

She nodded, her expression firming. "I'm going to do better." She turned to the corpse and began riffling through the pockets, pausing only brief to ask, "He isn't going to be turned in to the police, right? There's no need to guard my fingerprints?"

"You're fine. The Council of Guilds won't be concerned with him."

"Good. But we need to tell them about the explosion so that they can start to evacuate the city."

"I'll send Miranda to alert them to the threat, but so far, we only have your vision as proof."

She frowned. "They won't believe me?"

"Some will. Some won't. And even if they do, there are many people in Guild City who can't leave. They have magical ties to this place. Others won't blend in the human world. We could get many of them out, but not all."

"So it's up to us to stop this."

"With some help, maybe. But yes. Largely so."

Shadows flickered in her eyes as she nodded and turned back to searching the body. As she worked, I called Miranda on my comms charm and told her to go to the Council. They'd do what they could to mitigate this, if they believed us.

Carrow pulled a plain white napkin out of the man's pocket, a frown on her face. "This was the only thing on him."

"Try it."

She closed her eyes, and I felt her magic swell on the air. It smelled of lavender, and the scent was stronger than ever. I wanted to roll around in it.

I was no longer surprised by it, frankly.

"I see the interior of a bar. A posh one. There's writing behind the bar. *La Papillon.*"

Dread uncoiled within me. "Is the writing in gold script on top of a large, antique mirror?"

"Yes. You know it?"

"I do. It's in Romania."

"Where you're from?"

I ignored the question. Townsfolk speculated about my past, but I'd never confirmed it. "It's a popular meeting place for criminals."

"Looks too posh for criminals."

"Top criminals. Not the rabble."

"Oh, excuse me." She raised her brows. "I didn't realize there was a hierarchy."

"Oh, there most certainly is."

"Well, our bloke was there. And maybe he got his marching orders while meeting someone else. I think we should look into it."

Surprise flashed through me. "You would want to help?"

"Of course. This is my new home. And investigating crimes is kind of my thing, anyway." She pointed at me. "Not to mention, you need to help me with my magic. This is the perfect opportunity."

"Excellent." Pleasure flashed through me.

"Just give me one more moment." She lifted the man's shirt to check his skin.

"What are you looking for?"

"Any distinct marks."

She moved toward the short sleeves on his shirt, about to pull one up. I reached out to stop her, but she was too quick. She lifted the left sleeve, revealing an intricate tattoo that looked like the compass rose. North pointed toward the man's triceps, as if he were leaving it behind.

Shite.

"That's a strange tattoo," she murmured.

"It is." A familiar one, in fact. One I'd hoped she wouldn't see. One connected to my past. "Just a bit of pretty artwork."

Her gaze flicked to mine, suspicious.

Damnation. I'd laid it on too thick.

"How did you know he might be a threat to Guild City and not just your empire?"

"They're one and the same."

"Hmm." The suspicion didn't fade from her eyes.

"When you're done here, we'll need to prepare for a visit to La Papillon."

"Prepare?"

"Dress for it."

"What do you mean, dress for it?"

"You aren't with the police anymore, Carrow. We can't walk in there dressed in our street clothes."

She looked me up and down. "*Those* are your street clothes?"

"It's a casual suit. And we need to blend in to get our information."

"Hmm. I don't have any clothes that are posh enough for that place."

"That won't be a problem. I'll drop you at a shop that specializes in the kind of clothes you'll need."

"I also don't have any money." She grinned and shrugged.

"It won't be a problem. Tell the proprietress that it's on the Devil."

"Just like that? I don't need to give her a card or some fancy password?"

"That will do."

"Wouldn't people in town just charge stuff to you all the time?"

I laughed. "No, I'm not worried about that."

"They wouldn't dare, would they?"

"They wouldn't."

"All right then, but beware, I'm going to be expensive." Her eyes gleamed. "And I prefer to shop with friends. Mac is going to join me."

"Fine." She was going to ring up a serious bill, I could already feel it. I didn't mind a bit.

Carrow

The Devil walked me to a shop near his tower that looked like the poshest dress boutique I'd ever seen. I'd called Mac, and she was waiting for us when we arrived, leaning against an ancient tree that grew out of the pavement.

I turned to the Devil. "See you in an hour."

He nodded, then strode back toward his tower.

"What's going on?" Mac asked.

I looked at her, my brows raised. "We're going on a shopping spree."

"Really?"

"Yes. Which is the second reason I asked you here.

The first one is that I've got info. I wanted to be able to tell you, and this was the best way."

"Works for me. What's going on?"

I filled her in on the explosion, watching as her face went pale. "Really?" she said.

"Really. But we're going to stop it."

"Hell yes, we are."

"There's another thing, though. I don't trust the Devil."

"Good." She drew out the word in a way that implied that was the obvious thing.

"The guy on the table had a tattoo that the Devil didn't want me to see. And I still don't get how he knew that this guy was a threat to Guild City. He says that the city and his empire are one and the same, but..."

"It's too much of a coincidence."

"Exactly."

"And you're still going with him to this bar?"

"The alternative is Guild City blowing up, so yes."

"Fair enough. I'll ask around and see what I can find out about this, but I bet's its nil. The Devil keeps his business close to his chest."

"I can imagine."

"At the very least, I can snag a transport charm from Eve and be ready to come get you if something goes wrong in Romania."

"Thank you." Relief surged through me. Something deep in my soul told me that the Devil wouldn't hurt me. But the situation we were walking into was totally unknown and seemed to be related to magical criminal underworld dealings. I liked the idea of having a way out.

So, are we doing this or what?

Cordelia's voice sounded from down below, and I looked down to see the little raccoon. "You're coming with us?"

I'm always here for the good stuff.

"And the bad stuff." I thought of Black Church, of her worriedly watching from the shadows.

I looked at Mac. "Can Cordelia come in the shop?"

Of course I can!

"Don't sound so offended!" I said. "In the human world, raccoons aren't allowed in shops. They aren't even allowed in this country, in fact."

Cordelia huffed.

"She'll be allowed in this one," Mac said. "Guild City doesn't have restrictions like that. Too many familiars."

"What is this place?" I looked up at the sign, which read *Fae Couture.*

"The nicest shop in town, if you want a deadly dress."

"Deadly dress?"

"Yes. The Fae are known for their beauty and style. They use that to their advantage, along with their charm and quickness. Their guild tends to sell spy services and other types of physical intelligence gathering. Not all of them are spies, though. Some turn their talents towards shops like these where you can look your best and be your most dangerous."

"Interesting." I didn't understand entirely what she meant, but the proprietress of the shop had come to stand in the window and stare at us. "We've been gawking at her shop too long."

"Let's go in."

The door opened automatically in welcome. As I entered the airy space, birdsong hit my ears. It filtered through the rafters high above, making it sound like we were in a fairy glen. I looked up, spotting the colorful creatures.

I hope they're toilet trained.

I grinned down at Cordelia.

The Fae woman who stood to the side turned to us with a smile. "Welcome."

Her voice sounded at home with the birdsong, and it was impossible not to be impressed by her. For one, she was astoundingly beautiful, with dark hair and brilliant green eyes. Her pointed ears were studded with gems, and though I couldn't see her wings because she had them magically hidden, I could only imagine that they were stunning. The dress she wore was a liquid, glittery thing that fit her like a second skin.

"Are you in the market for a dress?" she asked.

"Two." I pointed to Mac. "One for each of us, on the Devil."

Her brows rose, interest gleaming in her eyes. "All right, then, let's get started."

She waved her hand, and three champagne flutes floated over from the back of the shop. Golden liquid gleamed within, bubbles rising toward the surface. A glass stopped in front of each of us, even Cordelia, who plucked it out of the air.

I took mine. "Thank you."

"But of course." She drifted toward the back of the shop. "Look around, but in the meantime, I'm going to gather a few pieces I think might suit you."

"Thanks." I sipped the champagne, enjoying the burst of bubbles and flavor. "This is a bit different from the secondhand shops where I normally go."

"Same." Mac gulped her champagne. "But I could get used to it."

Me too. Cordelia nimbly climbed onto a padded bench, her glass clutched in one hand. *I love a good fashion show.*

I looked around, wondering if anyone else was watching the raccoon. I'd grown used to her antics, but this was over the top.

Neither Mac nor the proprietress was paying attention, as if Cordelia were a totally normal part of life. Apparently here, she was.

I shrugged and turned to the shop, entranced by the beautiful fabrics. I liked my uniform of denim and leather, but I had to admit, I didn't *hate* the idea of a pretty, sparkly dress. I'd probably have worn them more often if I had any money or a place to go.

In the back of the shop, the Fae proprietress moved quickly through the racks, flicking her hands and making dresses rise of their own accord. Her magic smelled of flowers and tasted like honey.

"Her magic feels lovely," I murmured.

"You can feel it?" Mac asked.

I nodded. "Can't you?"

"No. She's got it locked down tight, like all of us do."

"Really?"

"Really. But you can sense it?"

"I can."

Mac whistled low. "That's something special. You must be very powerful if you can sense the magic people are trying to hide."

"I don't think I could do it before."

She turned to me, eyes widening. "Really? You think you're changing?"

I shrugged. "Maybe."

"Well, keep tabs on that. It's unusual."

I nodded, watching the woman choose more dresses. Her beauty was so ethereal. Eerie, almost. It dredged up a memory of the two Fae women I'd seen walking toward the necromancer's horrible ceremony last week.

"What's on your mind?" Mac whispered. "You look like you ate a bad apple."

"I was just thinking about the Fae women who were involved in the necromancer's creepy ceremony."

"They're locked up now."

"Yeah, but they didn't look evil, and neither does she. There wickedness wasn't obvious."

"It never is."

"But it means there could be people in Guild City who are involved in terrible things."

"Just like in the human world."

"Good point." I'd seen some awful stuff, but it seemed worse when you added something like death magic to the mix.

The dresses flew closer, floating through the air like glittering, silky ghosts to swirl around us. The proprietress came back and smiled. "I think these would suit either of you very nicely."

I couldn't decide which of the four circling me I liked best, the sparkly gold, the silky white, the gleaming pink, or the velvet blue.

"Where is the dressing room?" I asked.

"Dressing room?" The woman frowned, though she still somehow looked impossibly beautiful.

"She's not from around here." Mac looked at me. "Just pick one."

"Um...the gold one."

The Fae flicked her hand in a complicated movement, her magic flaring brightly. A moment later, I wore the dress, my champagne glass still in my hand.

"Ohhhh, nice!" Mac said.

I looked down, surprised. "That was amazing."

"One of the *many* perks of magic," Mac said.

"No kidding." It wasn't like I got to shop much, but I hated the trying-on process.

A mirror appeared in front of us, and I admired myself. "I look good."

"You're going to look even better," the Fae said.

I think you're perfect just the way you are.

I turned back to Cordelia. The raccoon had become a little kiss arse since I'd bought her a kebab from the place below my flat. "I know what you're doing."

She smiled innocently, the empty champagne glass clutched in front of her.

We tried on the rest of the dresses in no time flat. I ended up deciding on the gold one, while Mac got a silver number that made her look amazing.

"And what will you be wearing this for?" the Fae asked.

Mac pointed to me. "She's the one who needs the works."

"The works?" I was still wearing the gold dress, since I'd be going straight to La Papillon in it.

The Fae woman smiled. "Will you be on an assassin job? Intelligence gathering? A robbery?"

"Whoa, what?"

"She's going to enchant your dress, dummy." Mac

nudged me. "Tell her what you're doing. Not all the details, of course."

"There's confidentiality within these walls." The Fae leaned forward with a gleam in her eye.

I believed her. Not enough to tell her everything, though. "I'm going to a posh bar to find out information."

"Ooh." She tapped her chin. "Reconnaissance. Fun!"

She walked around me, humming to herself as she thought. Then she tapped my arm, and magic shot through the fabric, warming my skin.

"You can now have the strength of a heavyweight fighter," she said. "Two or three punches before the magic wears out, in case you get in a bad spot and need to slug your way out."

I inspected my arm. "Wow, thanks."

She tapped my back, and the entire dress warmed. "And now you'll be forgettable. Not during your encounters, mind you. You'll still be able to charm others into giving you information. But as soon as you walk away, it will be difficult for them to remember your face."

"That's amazing." My mind raced. "Can I be extra fast?"

"I can give you a bit of speed. Perhaps a couple other things."

"Give me the works, then. No expense spared." I pointed to Mac. "Her, too."

The Fae tapped me once again, and this time the

magic was slightly chilly. She did Mac next, giving her similar enchantments. I wasn't sure what Mac would do with her dress, but hopefully, she'd tell me the details later.

"Now, shoes!" The Fae woman moved to the back, and we followed.

She kitted us out with stilettos that felt like trainers and could make us graceful and agile, then moved on to jewelry, including a bangle that turned into blade and a pendant necklace that could hold hidden charms.

Makeup and hair came next at a little salon next door, and when we were done, we looked like a million quid and could charge that much on the black market as spies.

"Well, that was amazing," Mac said as we stepped out onto the street.

It was finally dark, and neither of us looked too out of place in our fabulous ensembles. The Devil waited for us, leaning against a tree in an impeccable slim-cut tuxedo that made him look like a posh killing machine. He was impossibly handsome with his dark hair and slate eyes. They seemed to heat when he looked at me, and I was reminded of the fire banked deep inside him.

I quirked an eyebrow at him, and he shifted, clearing his throat. "You look lovely. Both of you."

"Thanks, mate." Mac grinned cheekily and pointed at him. "Be careful with Carrow. Because I'll come for you if anything happens to her."

"I'd expect nothing less."

Mac nodded, then gave me a hug. "I'll see you later. I've got some business to attend to. But call me if you need anything."

"Thanks."

She skipped off down the street, and I turned to the Devil. "Do we leave from here?"

"Yes." He held out a hand, and I looked at it but didn't take it. "We're going to use a transport charm. It'd be better if you held my hand."

"You mean I'd be more likely to get to the right location?"

"Precisely."

I stepped forward and gripped his large hand, shivering as heat raced up my arm. His hand swallowed mine, and I tried not to enjoy the sensation. "How does it work?"

"It creates a temporary portal through the ether that responds to my wishes. The ether will transport us wherever I request."

"Oh, boy. That sounds...."

"Frightening?"

"Crazy." I looked down at my enchanted dress, which was something out of my wildest fantasies. "But crazy doesn't mean impossible, so let's go."

"Hold on tight."

His words rushed through me, and now that I had got hold of him, it amazed me how natural this felt.

6

Carrow

The Devil reached into his pocket and withdrew a small gray stone. He threw it to the ground right in front of us, and a cloud of silver smoke poofed up, glittering and bright.

"Come on." He tugged at my hand, and I followed him into the smoke.

An unseen force sucked us in and spun us through space. My stomach pitched like I was on a roller coaster, but a moment later, my feet hit solid ground.

Startled, I stumbled slightly. The Devil caught my arm, steadying me against him. Our bodies touched, and desire raced through me.

We hadn't been this close since he'd bitten me. My

gaze flashed to his, and I found him looking down at me. The heat in his eyes made me flush, and I pulled away, heart racing.

"You'll get used to ether transport." His voice was slightly hoarse, and I wondered if he was as affected as I was.

I thought so, but I shook the notion away and turned to inspect our surroundings. We stood on a street wide enough to allow cars by day but filled with people at night. Lovely historic buildings rose four stories high on either side of the street, their bottoms filled with shops and bars. Their smooth plaster fronts were painted different colors, and the roofs were made of lovely terracotta tiles. Many of the windows in the buildings were dark.

It was a lovely little city, but not what I'd have expected. I'd envisioned a bar somewhere in Paris or Tokyo or Bucharest.

"Is this the capital?" I asked. It seemed smaller than I'd have thought.

"No. It's Brașov, a city in Transylvania."

"Your home region?"

He ignored the question, but I was determined to figure out if he was Vlad the Impaler. He'd dodged the question every time before, and he was still doing it.

"Supernaturals prefer this region. It is full of magic and power. They've been here for hundreds of years.

Come." He gestured for me to follow, and I joined him, walking quickly toward an unassuming alley.

He entered the dark, narrow space. My heels clicked on the cobblestones, and I avoided cigarette butts as we passed beneath dim lamps to a little courtyard hidden between two of the buildings.

"You're sure this is the right way?" I passed two men who stood against the wall, smoking.

"I am." He turned and passed through an arch, climbing a set of stairs. I followed, joining him on the next floor. A plain brown door waited, and he knocked in a peculiar rhythm.

A moment later, it swung open, revealing a stone-faced man in a black tux. Behind him, I caught flashes of the most fabulous bar I'd ever seen.

Wow.

We were here.

The man nodded to the Devil, his gaze flickering with knowledge, and then he stepped back to admit us.

We entered silently, the Devil not acknowledging the doorman. I followed his lead and quickly took in our surroundings.

It was a gorgeous place, large and high ceilinged, with dim lighting provided by glittering chandeliers. Ebony tables gleamed beneath them, and the red velvet chairs looked like something out of an old movie from the thirties or forties. There were nooks and booths scattered along the sides, providing perfect secret places to do dangerous business.

The bar stretched along the back, a gleaming silver affair staffed by a pair of twins—two dark-haired women identical in every way.

I started to walk toward them, determined to get to the bottom of things, but the Devil's hand gripped my arm gently. "Whoa, there."

I looked back at him, startled.

"Subtle, remember?" he said.

"Right." We clearly did business in different ways. He was all about sticking to the shadows and slipping information out of people. I was more of a charge-up-and-get-it-done kind of person.

Except it hadn't worked well for me back in the real world. I'd ended up expelled from Police College and arrested for murder.

So....

Yeah, I could try things his way.

"Come, we'll get a table." He tucked my hand into the crook of his arm like we were on a date, and I followed. He leaned down and murmured, "Just play along."

I shivered at the warmth of his breath against my skin and nodded.

People stared at us as we navigated the room. *Everyone.*

Did I really look that fabulous?

No.

I looked damned good, no doubt about it. But there were half a dozen women here who looked like supermodels.

People were staring at the Devil with the kind of avid interest usually reserved for celebrities and top-profile criminals.

In the magical world, it seemed he was both. Particularly here in Transylvania. There was a lot to this man that I didn't know, and with every second that passed, I was sure he knew more about the dead guy than he let on.

I scanned the room, catching sight of several bulky men. Guards, I assumed. Each sported a perfect, identical suit over a muscular body. Their eyes were cold and determined.

The Devil was right about blending in before we pounced for info. We needed to lull them into thinking we were just on a date.

He took us to the best table in the place, one set away from the crowd in its own alcove. The walls were made of windows that allowed a fabulous view of the Eiffel tower.

"I thought we were in Brașov?" I asked.

"We are. It's an illusion."

"Wow. That's phenomenal." I felt like I could break through the glass and *be* in Paris.

"It changes daily, but I think the owner is partial to

Paris."

"You come here often?" *Yes.* An opportunity to dig.

"Not anymore."

"Oh?" I tried to sound disinterested as I sat in the tiny but comfortable chair. "Why not?"

"That's as much as you're getting."

"Fine." I looked around, inspecting other patrons with what I hoped was vague interest. In fact, I was ravenous for details.

"We'll get a drink and see if you can glean anything with your magic," he said.

"Right here?"

"Why not?"

"What if he didn't sit at this table? We can't sit at all of them."

"It will be good practice. And we need to sit for a bit and pretend to be here for a drink before we can go scouting for info."

A server in a perfect black minidress approached. Before she reached the table, the Devil held up two fingers, and she nodded and disappeared.

I gave him an appraising look. "You might not have been here in a while, but they seem to know your order."

"Indeed." He didn't elaborate, and I found myself desperate for more info.

The server returned moments later with a bottle of champagne and two flutes. Silently, she poured, then disappeared like a ghost. I had no eye for wine labels, but my first taste told me that this was the good stuff.

"Now, practice," the Devil said. "Or we'll save the city, and you'll *still* end up in the dungeons of Black Church."

I scowled at him. "I'll get control of my magic."

"Good. Show me."

I drew in a steadying breath and rested my hand on the table, feeling the rich cloth beneath my fingers. Visions of people sitting here flashed in my mind, but none of them were our guy.

"I don't see him," I said.

"Can you ask a specific question?"

"I can try, but it doesn't always work."

"Let me help."

My gaze flicked up to his. "How?"

"May I touch your arm?"

"Um, yes?"

His fingertips rested lightly against my bare forearm, a simple touch, but I liked it—too much. Magic buzzed over my skin. *His* magic.

I shivered. "What are you doing?"

"Think of it as a transfer of power. I'm giving you some of my control. The connection will help you find your own."

"Wow." My head felt woozy. We were bound in some cosmic way, two stars spinning through space. I'd suspected we were linked, and this confirmed it.

There was more to it than just magic, though. I could feel his inherent goodness, somehow. It wasn't strong or overwhelming—maybe it was even a product of my imagination—but I could feel it.

I looked up at him. "I sense the kindness in you. You're not all bad."

"You have no idea what I've done." The shadows in his voice made me shiver. "The atrocities you imagine that Vlad the Impaler committed? Worse. Ten times worse."

I swallowed hard and looked away.

"Focus," he ordered.

I blinked, trying. Work was safer than he was.

Visions flashed through my mind, and I tried to hone in on one in particular, a woman with dark hair who'd sat here last.

"It's working," I said.

"Good. Focus on the feeling of control. On where your magic is coming from inside you. It will help you in the future."

I nodded, doing as he said. "It's easier this time, but our guy never sat at this table."

"That's fine." He withdrew his hand, and I felt the strangest sense of loss. "We'll approach the bar under the pretense of wanting to taste some local wines, and we can ask the bartender."

"All right." I stood, leaving my emptied champagne glass on the table. I hated to leave the rest of the bottle, but there was no way I could drink more and still take care of myself, even with this enchanted dress. "Let me use the facilities, and I'll join you."

He nodded.

I turned and strode toward the toilets, finding them without too much trouble. As I passed the men's room, I trailed my hand along the wooden door. Had our guy touched it? I used my new control to focus on the faces, but there were too many, a jumble of images I couldn't decipher.

I headed to the women's room, determined to practice more. Another patron was standing at the sink when I entered. Her eyes met mine in the mirror, and she gasped.

"You!" she said, her accent light and unfamiliar.

"Me?"

She turned to face me, swaying slightly and clearly a little bit tipsy. "You're with *him*."

"The Devil of Darkvale."

"Yes." She nodded, her tone wary.

"I am."

"Be careful. He is not what he seems."

"I've been getting that impression. But who is he?"

"He's...you know." She looked around as if to check that the room was empty. It was so silent that it had to be. "The Impaler."

A chill raced through me. "Really?"

"Really."

Did I believe her?

Yes.

I'd already known it, even though he'd never confirmed it. And now I was dead certain.

She was obviously worried about me. Concern radiated from her like perfume. She'd clearly had enough to drink that her guard was down.

"Just be careful." Her voice was intense. "He has a terrible past here."

"But it's *in* the past?"

"Yes. Long ago, but... those things cannot be forgotten."

The chill on my skin grew colder. "Thank you for the warning."

She nodded. "I can show you the back way to sneak out, if you want."

"Thank you, but I can't. I am with him for a reason tonight, but I'll be careful, I swear."

She nodded, looking unsurprised, and left.

I watched her leave, her pink dress glittering under the light, and was struck again by the thought that drunk girls were the best people on earth.

As I finished my business and tidied up at the sink, I thought of the Devil. Of his many secrets. Of the goodness I'd felt in him when he'd shared his magic with me. But he'd also told me that he was worse than I could imagine.

Which one was the real man?

7

THE DEVIL

Carrow emerged from the corridor. She glowed with an ethereal light that drew me to her, the most beautiful woman I'd ever seen.

I leaned back against the bar and waited for her. The bartender had asked what I wanted when I'd first approached, but I'd made an excuse. I would wait for Carrow. We would need both of our skills for this.

My gaze followed her as she walked across the room. So did the gaze of every other man.

I clenched my fists, fighting back the desire for violence.

Rational thought pulled me from the precipice. I'd left that part of my life behind. I needed to atone. At the very least, I could refrain from tearing other people's heads off. I was a pastime I'd once enjoyed, but my cold, dead heart recognized it as wrong.

Mostly.

Carrow stopped in front of me. She was close enough now that I could see the shadows in her gaze.

"Are you all right?" I asked.

"Fine."

Despite her small smile, there was something under the surface. Mistrust?

I couldn't blame her. I wouldn't trust me, either.

But this seemed newer. Deeper.

"Let's do this." She moved her gaze to something behind me.

I turned as the bartender approached. She had nondescript features and cunning eyes. Intelligence gleamed in their depths.

"What can I get you?" she asked.

Her twin was nowhere to be seen, which made this the perfect time to act.

I leaned close and pitched my voice low, giving it all my magic. "We are looking for any information on this man."

I pulled the picture from my pocket and showed it to her.

Her gaze blurred at the sound of my voice. She blinked at the image. "I don't recognize him."

The words sounded forced from her. "Don't try to lie."

"I'm...not."

"You are." I pulled the magic from deep inside me and sent it pulsing toward her. It was invisible, but I often imagined it as smoke that they inhaled.

My compulsion hit her, and her eyes became totally unfocused. "He met Ivan here several days ago."

The name punched me in the stomach, but I wasn't unsurprised. The old bastard was back. "What did they discuss?"

"I couldn't hear them."

This, I believed. Ivan, a notorious warlord from my past, was clever and careful. I'd put him in the ground centuries ago, but he'd risen, it seemed, and kept all his talents.

Carrow's hand crept out. She rested her fingertips against the woman's forearm and closed her eyes. I felt her magic swell, the scent of lavender rushing over me. I held my breath, not wanting to inhale the sweetly spicy scent for fear of losing my focus.

"They sat on the other side of the room, across from us," Carrow said. "Too far for her to hear. But she saw them pass something between them."

"Was it a napkin?" I asked.

"No."

The bartender struggled to break free, but I pushed more magic toward her.

"It was a key," said Carrow.

"A key? To what?"

"I don't know." There was truth to her words.

The bartender's twin approached from the other side of the bar, returning from her errands. Her sharp eyes narrowed on us, and she strode over, a scowl cutting deep across her face.

I withdrew my power from the air, calling it back to me. Carrow jerked her hand back, but it was too late.

"You are not welcome here," the angry twin said.

The bartender gasped and glared at us. She raised her hands and gestured, and a band of men stepped from the shadows. No surprise. I'd spotted them when we'd walked in. Perhaps they were Ivan's men, set to guard his old favorite hangout in his absence.

Fine. I wanted Ivan to know we were coming for him.

After all, he was coming for me.

Carrow

I turned from the bartenders, spotting the huge men drifting away from the walls. The guards I'd noticed earlier.

"Are you ready to use that dress?" the Devil asked.

I nodded, shaking out my right arm and hoping that the punching charm worked.

The Devil murmured against my ear, "We need to get to the exit, and we can't transport out of here because of a protective charm."

"I got it."

Tension prickled across my skin.

The men charged—at least eight of them, maybe more.

The Devil was faster. His movements were a blur, his vampire speed incredible. Within seconds, he'd knocked together the heads of two of the guards. They collapsed like redwoods, unconscious.

I left him to it, racing for the door. I'd fight if I had to, but I wasn't going to run straight at the guys like he did. Let him take the worst of the hits.

My enchanted stilettos gave me Fae agility with the comfort of trainers. I darted around tables with speed and grace. I was nearly halfway to the door when a tall, dark-haired man intercepted me. A small, black table stood between us. I grabbed it and swung it at him, and the legs broke against his chest.

He growled and reached for me. I shoved the wreckage of the table at him and dodged behind him. When I kicked him in the knee, he went down hard. Sprinting around him, I punched him in the face. The blow landed with a force that shocked me. He grunted, spit and teeth flying.

"Holy crap." I spun around, adrenaline keeping me moving. Another guard hurtled toward me. I tried to avoid him, but he was fast. He grabbed me, yanked me against his chest, and wrapped a beefy arm around me.

Across the room, I saw the Devil dispatch four men, but more were coming at him.

I was on my own.

I flicked my wrist, converting my bangle into the dagger like the Fae woman had shown me. The hilt fit easily in my hand. I stabbed over my shoulder, hoping to hit something fleshy.

The knife hit its mark. The guard roared and shoved me forward. I stumbled but kept my grip on my blade, then righted myself and spun around.

"You want to play it that way, do you?" He withdrew a knife from inside his suit coat. It was easily twice as long and scary as mine.

Crap.

He darted toward me, swiping out with speed and precision. The steel sliced my arm, and pain flared. I yelped and leapt back, taking stock of my surroundings. There was another table, but it was too far away.

The man advanced, bloodlust in his eyes.

I'd never been any good at throwing knives, but I was desperate. I chucked mine at him, praying.

Somehow—by magic or luck or unknown skill—the blade pierced his shoulder. He roared, momentarily stunned. I lunged forward and punched him hard in the face, grateful for my magical Fae clothing.

Just like before, the man's head jerked sideways, and two teeth flew out.

He teetered in front of me. I yanked my dagger out of his shoulder and sprinted for the door, leaping over a fallen chair and swerving around a table.

Out of the corner of my vision, I caught sight of the Devil. He punched the last guard standing and sprinted for me. I increased my speed. Thanks to the shoes, I was fast, if a bit awkward. I reached the door just as the host stepped out of an alcove.

The polite man who had welcomed us to the club was gone. He now bore the fiery eyes and furrowed brow of someone out for blood. He raised a massive spiked club, and I skidded to a stop just out of range.

The Devil hurtled past me, fast and powerful as a freight train. The other man swung the club, but the Devil caught it in one hand. He took a spike to the palm without flinching and slammed his fist into the man's jaw, sending him toppling backward.

Blood dripping, he pulled his hand free of the club and stepped around the body. "Come on." He yanked open the door, and I sprinted through it, racing down the stairs.

He hurtled after me, and I looked back to see if any guards were following. There were none.

For now.

"They'll recoup and follow." The Devil held out his hand for mine.

I grabbed it, and he pulled a stone from his pocket, smearing blood on his trousers. He threw the thing to the ground, and the familiar silver smoke poofed upward. When he dragged me into the vapor, my stomach pitched as the ether spun me through space.

My feet met solid ground, and I stumbled. Gasping, I pulled my hand away from the Devil's and looked around. "This isn't Guild City."

In fact, it looked like the same town. There were the same beautiful four-story buildings and cobbled main street, along with the scent of the mountains and the cool breeze.

"It's not. We're staying here." He pointed to the gorgeous building in front of me. *The Crescent Hotel* was written in gold over the white exterior. "Come. We should get off the street before someone sees us."

I followed him up the stairs and into the fabulous lobby. It was gorgeous, with a marble floor gleaming under the sparkling light of two crystal chandeliers.

The huge wooden desk was manned by a beautiful woman with sleek red hair and a bright expression. Her eyebrows rose when she spotted us, and she inclined her head. "Welcome, Devil."

"Thank you. The rooms are ready, I presume?" The Devil's words were so smooth and cultured that I couldn't believe it was the same man who'd just torn through a room full of guards like a lion going after a steak buffet. His hand was dripping blood on the floor, but the hotel clerk studiously ignored it.

She hurried out from behind the desk and waved for us to follow. "I will show you straight to your rooms."

We followed her through the lobby and up a lift done in mahogany and gold accents. Within a minute, we were ensconced in a beautiful suite with a view overlooking the city and mountains beyond. Moonlight gleamed brightly over the scene.

"Please ring if you need anything." The woman disappeared.

I turned to the Devil. "You were prepared."

"I thought we might need to stay to learn more information."

"Hmm." Again, I got the feeling that he knew more about this than he was letting on.

His gaze flicked over me, and concern flashed on his face. "Your arm."

Fresh pain blazed. I looked down at the gash made by the guard's dagger. Adrenaline had driven it from my thoughts, but the Devil's words reminded me.

"Ouch." I resisted clapping a hand over it like I might with a smaller cut. This was ghastly. "I might need treatment for this."

"I can take care of it."

I looked at him, surprised. "What? Really?"

He nodded.

"You're not a nurse. Or a doctor."

"No. But I have healing powers."

"Oh." I blinked. "Like what?"

"Come here." He gestured for me to step closer.

"Tell me what you're going to do." I looked at his bleeding hand. "Strike that. Fix yourself first, and then I'll know what's coming."

"Mine will close on its own. Vampire blood has healing properties."

He was right. As I watched, the wound appeared to be growing smaller.

"I promise I won't hurt you," he said.

I could hear the truth in his voice, and my wound stung like hell.

"Are there any side effects?"

"No."

I drew in an unsteady breath and approached him.

His gaze dropped to the dripping wound, and his nostrils flared. His jaw tightened, and his eyes flashed. There was something hot and dark and unreadable in his stare.

My heartbeat picked up the pace. "What's wrong?"

"Nothing." His voice was tense, and I swore I could see the slightest bit of his fangs, which were normally retracted. He looked away, his jaw working as he got himself under control.

Was he turned on?

Was I crazy for thinking that?

But his eyes...

I shivered. "Is it my blood?"

He nodded sharply. "This hasn't happened in...ever."

I swallowed hard. "But there's something between us."

His gaze moved back to mine. Heat crackled between us like lightning. "There is."

Cursed Mates.

I didn't say it. I couldn't. Tension had stolen my voice.

"I won't bite you without your permission," he said, his voice rough.

"I know." Did I, though? Fear shot through me, followed by desire. "Just heal me, okay?"

Excitement had me thrumming. I couldn't help it.

He nodded sharply and raised his wrist to his lips. His fangs were out. At the sight of them, something inside me warmed.

He sunk them into his wrist. I winced, but he didn't so much as flinch. He raised his head. Two pearls of blood had formed on his wrist.

He held his arm to my lips. "Don't drink, just lick."

Shock raced through me. "*What*?"

"You won't turn into a vampire, but my magic needs to get into your system. Born vampires would anoint the wound with their blood, but I am turned." His gaze flicked to my lips. "This works better with our kind."

"Um..." My gaze dropped to his wrist, and heat flashed through me.

I felt like an inferno, a blazing desert storm.

My human side rebelled. This was crazy.

The magic side of me leaned closer, drawn by the intoxicating scent of his magic and the crimson liquid that beckoned.

I swiped my tongue over his wrist. The flavor made my head spin.

A low, rough groan was torn from his throat, a sound so faint I almost didn't hear it. I lifted my gaze. His head was tipped back, and his eyes were squeezed shut, as if he were in pain.

Or pleasure.

He acted as though he hadn't been touched in centuries, and he wasn't sure if he liked it.

"Does it hurt?" I asked.

"No." The roughness in his voice was like a caress.

I shivered and stepped closer to him.

He straightened and opened his eyes. The pupils were dark and blown out. "Careful."

"Of what?"

"Me."

We were so close that I could feel the heat of him. I could smell his fireside scent and see the pulse at his neck. His touch earlier tonight had shown me how good he was. Deep down, at least.

He wouldn't hurt me.

"Don't think that," he said.

"What?"

"That I won't hurt you."

"How did you know?"

"I can see it in you. Your trust. You can't trust me not to hurt you."

"You won't." And he wouldn't—not on purpose. I could almost *feel* his restraint, like a physical thing on the air.

For the first time, I wondered if he was torn about his species. If he didn't like it. He was so complex, the Devil.

I had to touch him. I couldn't help it. Maybe it was his magic racing through my system. Maybe it was just him.

But I had to.

There was something dangerous between us. Something I didn't understand.

And I didn't care.

I rested my hands on the wide planes of his chest, the warmth of his skin burning my palms and shivering up my arms. My gaze moved up to his lips in time to see them part on a groan.

His big hands came up and gripped my waist, pulling me to him. His touch was forceful, commanding.

I loved it.

The low groan reverberated in his throat as his lips pressed warm and hard against mine. Sparks exploded behind my eyelids as I parted my lips and welcomed the slick glide of his tongue. His fangs had retracted, and his kiss was nothing but pleasure.

I wrapped my arms around his neck as he crushed me to him, pressing the full length of my body against his. Every inch of him was against me, hard and unforgiving.

His hands moved down my sides, strong and firm, as if he couldn't get enough of me. Broad palms cupped my hips and pulled me closer. His lips moved from my mouth to my neck, as if he wanted to taste all of me.

When I felt the slight scrape of his fangs against my skin, I jerked, startled.

He was faster, pulling away from me, horror in his eyes. "I'm sorry."

"You didn't do—"

"I didn't control myself. I *couldn't.*" I could hear the loathing in his voice.

"So the biting and sex are..."

"Not linked. Not normally." His gaze moved over me, something unreadable in its depths. "But with you... I said you shouldn't trust me."

I rubbed my arms, still hot from his touch yet chilled with worry. Maybe he was right—maybe he was dangerous.

I still wanted him.

"Don't look at me like that." His words were soft.

"Like what?"

"Like you want me." He raked a hand through his hair. "It's hard enough to resist you."

I wanted to scoff that it wasn't true, but I couldn't.

He turned away from me. The movement seemed to cost him an effort. "In the morning, we'll search for more clues about Ivan's plans. For now, you need rest. There's another bedroom."

"Um...okay." I walked away from him, knowing it was for the best. But as I headed toward the other room, my heart pounding, I couldn't forget the feeling of his lips—his fangs—against my skin.

8

Carrow

In the other bedroom, my mind still spun. I couldn't believe that anything could feel like that.

And what I'd almost done.

Everything.

I'd have given him anything he wanted.

Breathing hard, I went into the bathroom and washed my face. I could hear the Devil's shower going in the other room and couldn't help but think of him in there.

"No." I stared into the mirror, taking in my wild eyes and wilder hair. "Bad Carrow. Get your mind out of the gutter."

But it so badly wanted to *be* in the gutter.

I shook my head and stripped out of the dress and shoes, staying in the bra and panties that the Fae woman had given me. They didn't have any powers, but they sure were pretty. I needed a shower, but honestly, what I really needed was a drink.

Shaking slightly, I walked into the room to find something to calm my nerves. What I wouldn't give for a box of wine and Cordelia. Not that I wanted to go back to my regular life, but hell, this new life was getting *very* crazy.

In the minifridge, I found a small bottle of white wine and poured myself half a glass. This was not the time to lose my wits, but the wine tasted good going down. More than anything, I liked the ritual of it. The ability to focus on something besides my thoughts.

I headed back toward the bathroom, determined to take a quick shower and get a tiny bit of sleep.

A noise from the window made me jump. I turned, ice racing over my skin.

The window swung open, and an enormous man slipped into the room. I opened my mouth to scream, but he flicked his hand, and my throat closed tight. He approached quickly.

Panic flared.

Where was my dagger bracelet?

The other side of the room.

A weapon. I needed a weapon.

He was on me before I could move, as swift as the

Devil had been back in the bar. Except he wasn't fighting to protect me.

The intruder's hand closed around my throat. "You've been poking into things that are better left alone." His eyes gleamed with a cold, demonic darkness.

I kicked out at him, but we were too close. He tightened his grip.

The wine glass.

I smashed it against the wall and stabbed him in the neck with the broken stem. His eyes bulged. Blood bubbled up around the wound, but he didn't let go.

I struggled kicking and hitting, but he didn't so much as budge. Even the glass shoved into his throat didn't slow him.

My vision faded at the edges. Fear sliced through me, and my lungs burned. I kicked the wall behind me, hoping to alert the Devil, and clawed at the man's cheeks, raking gouges into the skin that made him grin eerily.

His face shifted, transforming into something rougher, with horns protruding from his head. Blood dripped from his neck wound, and his breath gurgled around it, but his grip on my throat didn't loosen.

Tears pricked my eyes.

Cordelia appeared out of the corner of my vision, and hope collided with fear. The little raccoon was no match for this monster.

She raced toward him anyway. She'd nearly reached

him when the Devil slammed into the room.

"Release her!" The Devil charged the monster who had me pinned.

Cordelia veered out of the way, and the Devil jerked the bastard off me. I coughed and went to my knees, sucking air through my burning throat. My hair fell over my face as I tried to catch my breath.

Through the strands, I saw a massive spray of blood paint the floor. Shocked, I looked up. The Devil held the monster's head in his hands.

The body lay on the floor.

Holy crap.

On the other side of the room, Cordelia disappeared, as if it were just too much for her.

Hell, it was too much for me. I might have magic, but I wasn't used to this magical world of vampires tearing off monster heads.

Throat still burning, I scrambled back against the wall.

Something strange flashed across the Devil's face, almost like shock or regret, and he tossed the demon head aside. It thudded to the ground.

Oh God, Police College had not prepared me for this.

"Are you all right?" He fell to his knees beside me, eyes dark with worry and lips tight.

I gasped, my lungs struggling to feed oxygen to my starved body. "Yeah. Thanks."

My unwilling gaze went to the head on the floor.

"I'm sorry about that." He frowned. "That was...gruesome."

"It's fine." As much as my stomach was heaving, it really was fine. That horned *thing* had been about to squeeze the life from me. I'd take his death over mine any day, and I'd learn to get the iron stomach necessary to live in this world.

"I try not to kill anymore, but when I saw you there..." He trailed off. "I lost it."

"You were worried?"

"Of course."

"Thanks."

He nodded, raising his hand as if to reach for me. He closed it into a fist and lowered it. "You're certain that you're all right?"

"I'll be fine."

"I should have let him keep his head. We could have questioned him."

"Maybe not. I shoved my wine stem in his throat. But why didn't he die? He could barely breathe."

"He's a demon. They need air, but their bodies are different. Some can go longer without oxygen."

I looked back at the body, which appeared to be flickering. "What's happening to him?"

"Shite." The Devil surged to his feet and approached the body. "Demon bodies disappear from this plane and reappear back in their hells."

"He's not really dead?"

"He is. For a while, at least."

The Devil knelt by the body and began to search the pockets. I blinked, realizing that he was half naked. He wore only his trousers, his entire top half bare.

I'd been so focused on his face a moment ago—on the fear for me that I'd seen there—that I hadn't noticed the rest of him. Now, I couldn't help but notice.

His muscles were chiseled to perfection, but his skin was a latticework of old scars. Knife and sword wounds, it looked like. Hundreds of battles from long ago. None of the bullet wounds one might see on a modern soldier.

A shadow on his shoulder caught my eye, and I squinted.

It looked like a compass rose, but far blurrier.

I scrambled upright and approached him silently, staring hard at it.

Holy crap—that was the same tattoo the corpse in his club had borne. The Devil had tried to have it removed, but it hadn't worked.

"What is that?" I demanded. "Your tattoo."

He stiffened, cursing slightly under his breath. "We need to search the body before it disappears."

He was right, but I was entranced by the tattoo. By the lies.

Then my training kicked in. I might have been tossed out of school, but I'd learned a hell of a lot. I shoved aside the emotion and stepped over the body, which was now half transparent. I could see the carpet beneath it as I knelt and began to search his jacket.

I pulled out everything I could, setting it on the ground beside me. Fueled by an idea, I jerked at the body's clothes, looking for the same tattoo the Devil wore.

I found it on the demon's shoulder.

I pressed my hand to it, calling on my magic. I had to know what it was.

The Devil's gaze burned into me as I tried, but nothing came. The bastard was too far gone. I looked up, searching for the head. I'd touch it if I had to—anything to get my answers.

But it was nearly gone, too.

I removed my hands from the demon. "You're going to tell me about your connection to this." The Devil's gaze shuttered, and I glared at him. "I'm not doing anything else until you tell me."

The body between us was nearly gone, and we were surrounded by a tiny collection of items that had been in the demon's pockets. A few colored stones that I now recognized as enchanted objects—charms, they were called—along with keys and a wallet, which seemed weird for a demon. But then, this whole world was weird.

"Carrow." The Devil's voice was heavy.

"You're going to tell me." I surged to my feet, and the Devil's gaze followed my movements. His jaw tightened.

Crap. I was still mostly naked.

The memory of our kiss flashed in my mind, and I shoved it aside.

"Don't look at me." I stomped to the bathroom and found a robe, then pulled it on.

When I returned to the room, the Devil was standing near the fridge, a glass of amber-colored liquid in his hand. He hadn't put on a shirt, and his front half was just as magnificent as the back. There were even more scars there, but somehow, they just emphasized his power and strength. I liked him more because of them, even as I was afraid of him.

He was impossibly handsome despite the shadows in his eyes. The slate gray had darkened, as if he were fighting off horrible memories, but I hardened myself against him.

"Well?" I demanded.

He sighed, then sat in one of the two chairs near the window. I joined him, perching on the chair across from him and nearly vibrating with anger.

"I didn't trust you when I agreed to help you," I said. "But this is worse than I expected."

"That's good." His voice was flat. "I'm far worse than you could ever expect."

"You're Vlad the Impaler, the famous vampire, right? And you murdered all those people." My gaze flicked back to the spot where the body had lay. "Why do you have the same markings as both of the bodies?"

"You know that I'm a turned vampire."

I nodded.

"Most vampires in the world are born. They're not much different than any other supernatural. They have magic, they're mortal. They're not monsters any more than witches or sorcerers or seers are. Some of them are evil, but it's not the nature of their species."

"But it is the nature of yours?"

"Some think so."

"*You* think so."

His entire dark history seemed to be reflected in his eyes. "It's hard not to. I own my actions, and I regret them."

"You killed those people?"

"Most of my worst deeds occurred in the past, shortly after I'd been turned."

I waited silently.

He leaned back and stared out the window. "Vampires are rarely made because few are capable of it. Few are *willing* to do it because their progeny—like me—become insatiable monsters, out for death and blood. They rampage across the countryside, killing anyone they come across."

I swallowed hard, horrified.

He continued. "Often, they don't live long. They're so out of control...so horrifically consumed by bloodlust... that they aren't good at covering their tracks. Vampire hunters take them out if others don't get to them first."

"You survived."

"I was strong and clever. For some reason, after I'd been turned, I retained parts of myself. My cunning, my charm." He shook his head, regret in every movement. "It makes it worse, somehow. That my mind was still partially there, even as I committed terrible atrocities."

"Did you like it?"

"Like it?" He met my gaze, confusion in his eyes. "I... don't know. I hated myself even then. Hated what I was doing. But I couldn't control it. The need would come over me like a black mist."

"Yet you survived," I said again.

"My skills helped me evade capture for years. Eventually, I created a small empire here in Transylvania."

All the myths were true, and I was sitting across from the man himself. The murderer.

I drew in a shaky breath. "What happened?"

"As the years went on, I shook off the effects of the turning. I was able to force the bloodlust down deep, far away to a place where it couldn't influence me. But before that happened, I made an alliance."

"With this Ivan."

"You're perceptive."

"It's the only direction this could possibly go."

"Ivan was worse than me, if possible. Not a vampire, but a mage out of control with power. Once I'd regained my senses, I no longer wanted to kill." His gaze met mine. "Don't think that means I'm not still a monster. I manipulate and threaten and compel others to get what I want. But I no longer murder senselessly."

"Oh, don't worry. I don't think you're a saint."

The corner of his lips quirked in a small, wry smile. "I don't know why I ever thought I had a chance at you."

Shock lanced me, and I stilled.

His gaze shuttered, as if he hadn't meant to say that. He continued speaking. "Ivan and I had a gang of supernaturals who fought for us." He touched his shoulder. "All were marked as I was. As Ivan was. The only way to stop them was to take out Ivan."

"But he's alive."

"Now he is. He was immortal—rare among supernaturals—and impossibly strong. Even harder to kill than I am. I incapacitated him and trapped him in a tomb at the bottom of the sea."

I could feel my eyes widen.

"I knew he'd be there a long time," he said. "But I'd hoped it would be for longer. It appears he managed to rise recently."

"And he's restarted your empire."

He nodded.

"But why attack Guild City?"

"To get back at me. He said he'd take everything I love."

"You love Guild City?"

"What else do I have?"

Shoot. He had a point. From what I'd seen, he lived a

shadowy, lonely life. Wealth and power of unimaginable scale, sure, but it wasn't a life I would want. Especially now that this Ivan was back from the dead. "Why didn't you tell me?"

"Would you want to tell the worst of your past?"

"If it was like yours, no."

Something flickered in his eyes, then was gone.

Had I hurt him?

I couldn't help but feel like I had. He didn't argue, though. How could he? His past *was* terrible.

"I'd already tried looking for Ivan myself," he said. "I couldn't check the tomb, but I had a feeling he'd returned. The leads ran cold, however. That's why I needed you."

My mind raced. "The man who broke into your club...was he a warning?"

"I think so, yes. It was a power play. Ivan's way of saying he had enough minions that he could throw them away."

"What a monster."

"You're sitting with one."

"You're not as bad as he is."

"But I was."

I didn't know how to respond to that—or even what I thought of it—so I stood and walked toward the objects on the ground. "We must find him and stop him. But how, if he's immortal?"

"If trauma can't kill him, I can contain him with

powerful magicuffs and imprison him again."

"Do you have magicuffs that are that strong?"

"There are some in the dungeons of Black Church that will work." The Devil stood and joined me.

At least we had a plan. We just needed to stop Ivan in time. I knelt by the objects and picked up a stone, hoping for information.

The Devil lowered himself to my side. "Do you need help?"

I remembered his touch at the bar, helping me control my magic. It had sent heat shivering through me, along with the sense of his inherent goodness.

Had that been my imagination? Wishful thinking?

Or had he partially reformed?

I shook my head. "Don't touch me."

If I really needed the help, I'd ask him. For now, I'd try on my own. I needed to keep my distance.

The stone was a transport charm. Somehow, I could feel it in the magic. There were two others, identical, but they provided no interesting information. "I'm keeping these."

The Devil nodded.

It was a small metal card that made me hesitate. I could sense the information in it, as if it might have belonged to someone important.

Maybe even Ivan.

I closed my eyes and focused my magic, gripping the card so tightly that it cut into my hands hard enough to hurt. I called on the magic inside me, remembering how I'd felt it deep in my soul.

The Devil's magic had helped me summon my powers. I tried to remember that feeling of connection as well and use it to my advantage.

The power burst out of me like water through a dam. My mind was filled with images, so many images that my vision dimmed. I dragged in a breath.

Find me information about the bombing.

That was my priority. Stopping the destruction of my new home.

As if on command, the visions swirled and narrowed to one—a small stone door with a symbol carved into it. I forced my vision outward, and it complied.

Shock and elation rushed through me at my new control. I'd never been this powerful before.

I saw multiple small stone doors, a crypt of some kind. But it was the one with the symbol on it that drew my attention, a twisted spiral with points, a unique design that throbbed with magic.

In my mind, I drew closer. The vision was so clear that it felt like I was *there*. But that was impossible.

I neared the symbol. Reaching out, I touched the stone.

My fingers made contact, and an enormous force blasted me backward. The shock sent waves of pain ripping through me, and I blacked out.

9

The Devil

I watched Carrow work, her eyes closed and her fingertips resting on the small metal card. Her magic pulsed on the air, flaring bright. The scent of lavender filled the room, followed by the sweet taste of oranges.

Stunned, I stilled. She was more powerful than ever. *Massively* so.

Something was changing in her. Something with her magic.

Pain twisted her face, and she slumped over, unconscious.

Fear rocketed through me, and I lunged for her, grabbing her before her head hit the hard floor.

"Carrow." I took her in my arms and brushed her hair away from her face. "Come on, Carrow."

Would I need to heal her?

I shuddered at the idea of her lips on my skin again.

Could I?

This wasn't a dagger wound or a broken bone. I had no idea how to deal with this.

Her eyes fluttered open, confusion flashing in their beautiful depths.

"What happened?" her voice was weak. Exhausted.

"Your power increased. I don't know how. I've never seen anything like it."

"What?" Her eyes blurred. "I'm so...tired."

Her eyes closed, and she fell asleep. I pressed my hand to her upper chest, wanting to feel her heartbeat. Her breathing came heavy and deep.

Asleep, not dead.

Exhausted by the extreme power that had blasted through her. I studied her face, looking for any sign of discomfort as my heart slowed.

She was all right.

I repeated it to myself like a mantra. The fear that had surged in me diminished, and I leaned back on my heels, cradling her to me.

She needed sleep.

I stood and carried her to the bed. Carefully, I laid her on the mattress and pulled the covers up over her.

Rubbing my chest at the strange sensation within, I rose and stared down at her.

What was happening to her?

What was happening to *me*?

A cold breeze drifted over me, and I turned, spotting the window that the attacker had opened.

This would not do.

I stalked over, pulled it shut, and locked it. The rooms should have been secured—that was one of the perks of this hotel. Once the locks were thrown on the doors and windows, no one could enter.

But this one had been unlocked.

I should have checked when I'd first come in, but I'd seen Carrow's wound, and then I'd had to heal her. And then...

The memory of her touch...her taste...nearly stole my mind again. I'd never felt anything like it.

And then she'd learned of my past...the whole awful, bloody lot of it. I'd reached too high when I'd reached for her. She was the first I'd wanted in centuries —the first that I'd *ever* wanted like this—and it could never be.

I went from room to room, checking all windows and doors. The rest were fine, but how the hell had that one been unlocked?

Did Ivan have contacts here?

Unlikely. This place and my fondness for it had developed after his time. He shouldn't know of it.

But I also couldn't be certain of the date he'd risen from the crypt at the bottom of the sea. Perhaps he'd been watching me for longer than I'd realized.

My gaze flashed to Carrow, who lay still, asleep and recovering.

He could never know about her.

He'd want her for her power as surely as I did.

Yet I wanted her for far more than that. The way she made me feel....

Alive.

Thawed.

Just like the Oracle had said. The Prophecy that I'd long believed was bullshit could be true. But what did it mean? Where did it go from here?

I walked toward Carrow, confusion racing through me.

She'd given me my senses back, a taste of life. But at what cost?

If there was one thing I'd learned in my long life, it was that everything had a price. Every sunny day was paid for with rain, every moment of joy with one of grief.

It was balance.

I spun away from her and strode to the other side of the room, speaking quietly into the comms charm at my wrist. "Miranda? Get the Oracle. Send her to me at the Crescent Hotel."

"Yes, sir. Though I can't guarantee she'll see you."

Miranda had a point. The Oracle was notorious for disappearing and not showing up to meetings. But she'd been so interested in Carrow and me that I had a feeling she might make an exception. "Just try."

"On it."

"Oh, and Miranda? How did the Council take the news of the possible explosion?"

"Some believed, some didn't. Witches are with you, sorcerers are not. Each guild is handling it for themselves."

"Keep working on them."

"Will do. Good luck."

I disconnected the comms and turned to watch Carrow.

A few minutes later, there was a brief knock on the door in the adjoining suite. I strode toward it, leaving the door to Carrow's suite open so that I could hear if she stirred.

I found the ephemeral figure of the Oracle on the threshold. Her face flickered from old to young, and she gave me a knowing smile.

"Finally interested in knowing more?" she asked.

"Yes."

"So you've decided it's not just bollocks, then?"

I shrugged, remembering how I'd initially written off her assertion that Carrow would thaw me and cure my immortality. "I'd like to know more."

"Hmm." She sauntered in. "Can't say I'm surprised."

I moved toward the middle of the room, where I could keep an eye on Carrow. "Speak quietly, please. Carrow is sleeping."

The Oracle's brows shot up. "My, my. You make quick work of things."

"It's not what you think. And I thought you were omniscient."

"No one is omniscient, and I don't make a point of spying on people's sex lives."

"That's big of you."

"I'm a saint."

"Tell me about this thawing and immortality situation with Carrow. What does it mean? How does it happen?"

"That, I do not know."

"What *do* you know?"

"She's your Cursed Mate."

Cursed Mate.

A memory flickered of long ago. I'd been toward the end of my bloodlust, still a murderous bastard but at least partially in control of my mind and body. Dread unfurled within me. "I thought that was a myth."

"Perhaps it is." She shrugged. "But likely not."

"What is it?"

"Depends on the mates. As you know, born vampires have fated mates. Turned vampires are said to have Cursed Mates. Few turned vampires survive long enough to find their mates, so little is known about them."

"It sounds bad."

"It does, doesn't it?" She raised a brow. "I think it's a mystery you'll have to solve."

"You can't help? You're the Oracle, for fates' sake! You should be able to see these things."

"I will look for you, but I cannot promise what I will see."

"You seem to be able to see what suits you."

"And that's fortunate for me."

"I'll pay you whatever you want." *Cursed Mates.*

It had to be bad. Deadly, even.

What had felt like a gift with Carrow—her blood returning my full senses and the connection I felt to her—was possibly a nightmare.

Given the way my life had gone, it likely *was* a nightmare. I hurt everything I touched. It was no surprise that I would have a Cursed Mate and hurt her, too.

I dragged a hand over my face, waiting for the Oracle to name her price. "Well?"

"I'll let you know if I come up with something. Then I'll charge you."

"Fine. Thank you." I nodded sharply, waiting for her to leave.

She vanished. I turned to Carrow's room, frustration pulsing through me. One of the most powerful oracles in the world had just delivered opened-ended terrible news, then disappeared. I'd have to find out more about this Cursed Mate situation, but not tonight.

Tonight, I needed to watch over Carrow.

I walked toward the bed and took a seat in the chair next to it, leaning back to guard her.

Carrow

Groggy, I shifted within a cocoon of soft sheets, blinking against the shaft of sunlight that shone across my eyes. I opened them, my vision clearing. The Devil was seated in a chair near the bed, watching me wearily.

Affection rushed through me.

"How do you feel?" His voice was slightly rough.

"Fine. What are you doing there?"

"Sitting."

"Weird." I sat up, my head spinning at the movement.

Memories rushed back. Last night, my vision, his tattoo. His secrets.

The affection vanished, and I shifted away from the Devil, glaring at him. "Why did you sit there all night?"

He shrugged. "You needed sleep, and I didn't think we should let down our guard."

"Oh." That was...nice.

I ignored it. I didn't know how to process *nice* right now. Especially not from him. Not when there was so much happening.

I pulled the bathrobe closer around me. "My vision was different."

"I could tell."

"How?"

"You passed out. And your magic surged like I've never felt. Something about it is changing."

I nodded. "I could control it. Zoom around inside the vision like I was controlling a video game. It was...wild."

"It's not greater control, Carrow. I could feel your power growing. Your *capacity* for it."

"Isn't that supposed to be finite? Every supernatural is born with a certain amount of power, and they learn to control it, for better or worse?"

"Normally, yes. You're different."

Huh. I was a weirdo even here, in the magical world. "Is that why the Council of Guilds was so hard on me?"

"It's probably why the ceremony couldn't place you in a guild, yes. It didn't recognize what you were."

"What I am? I read objects."

"Which possibly makes you a seer. Or not. It's a strange talent, not a normal seer gift."

"Crap." I needed to get to the bottom of that, but we had more important matters to deal with. "My vision showed a tomb. A crypt or mausoleum, I'm not sure. And there was a symbol on it. A spiral with points."

He reached for the bedside table and picked up the paper and pen that was ubiquitous in such places, apparently even in magical hotels. He passed them to me.

I took them and set about drawing the symbol. When it was as good as I could get it, I showed it to him.

He frowned and took it, studying it intently. "I don't recognize it."

"Neither do I." I looked toward the table on the other side of the room, where I'd put my mobile when I'd undressed. The gown had contained a special pocket for it. Hopefully, the battery would still have a charge. "I'm going to text a picture to Mac. Maybe she can figure it out."

He retrieved the phone and handed it to me. Quickly, I snapped a pic of the symbol and sent it to Mac. The Devil took the paper and did the same, then he pressed a finger to the comms charm on his wrist and spoke into it, telling Miranda to get started on research.

"You use a phone *and* a comms charm?" I asked.

He nodded. "The comms charm is easier for certain people, but only a couple are hooked up to this one. And there's no easy magical way to send a picture unless you're a sorcerer or a mage. Humans have got that one on us."

I nodded, searching my mind for memories of the vision. "I think that symbol is meant to play a role in the explosion. When I was seeking information about what the intruder was after, it showed me that. I think he may have been part of the team that was sent there, until he was rerouted here, to attack us."

"Do you know where the symbol is located?"

"Not precisely, no. But I did get the sense that it was in or near Guild City."

He nodded. "That will make it easier for Miranda to find it. You said it was a crypt? Could it be inside a church?"

"Maybe. Or a mausoleum or other burial chamber. I don't know what you supernaturals do with your dead." I winced as soon as the word came out of my mouth, reminded of the necromancer.

"You're one of us now."

"Right." I was grateful for the distraction. "But I still don't know what happens to dead people in Guild City. Are there a lot of crypts?"

"There are some. Graveyards, too. Churches. It's not terribly dissimilar from what humans do."

"All right." I climbed out of bed. "We need to find that crypt."

My phone dinged, and I looked down to find a message from Mac.

Will get right on it. Text me when you're back.

. . .

I responded that I would, then looked at the Devil. "I'm going to get a quick shower, then let's head back to Guild city. We only have two nights left to stop this."

He nodded. I left him, managing not to look over my shoulder.

I made quick work of the shower, thought I desperately wanted to linger. I'd never been in such a nice one —the one in my old London flat had been terrible, and the one in my new place was fine, but tiny and fitted into an ancient building.

This was pure luxury, and I had to race through it.

By the time I returned to my room, I found a set of clothes laid out on the bed. They looked like my normal clothes, but they weren't. I frowned at them and shouted toward the Devil's room, "These aren't my clothes!"

"They are now."

"How?"

"I had them delivered."

Hmm. Thoughtful. I dressed quickly and gathered up my discarded gown and shoes. The magic in them might be mostly used up, but it was still a hot dress. I could wear it to the next Witches' Masquerade. Anyway, I'd never had anything quite so nice before, and I wasn't about to give it up.

I checked my phone and found a message from Mac.

Meet us at the Haunted Hound. Eve may have something.

. . .

I found the Devil in his room, dressed in all-black tactical wear, not dissimilar to what his security detail wore. Which reminded me…

"Why didn't we bring your security yesterday?"

"It was supposed to look like a date. I didn't want to trigger the guards before we got our information."

"And your new look?" Which, I hated to admit, suited him pretty damned well.

"I have a feeling things are about to get a lot more active. Better to be prepared."

"Hmm. Ready?"

He nodded and held out his hand. I strode over to him and gripped it, unable to help the shiver that ran through me. I still wanted him. I didn't trust him, but I couldn't help my physical awareness of him. The connection that drew us together like a wire.

Cursed Mates.

I shoved the thought away. I'd figure out exactly what that meant later.

"Let's go to the Haunted Hound Pub. Mac told me that Eve might know something," I said.

"All right." The Devil drew a transport charm from his pocket and threw it to the ground. The silver smoke poofed up, and I followed him inside, growing more used to the pull of the ether.

10

CARROW

The ether spat us out in Guild City at the gate leading to the Haunted Hound.

“Is there a reason that your friends prefer to meet in the middle ground between Guild City and the human one? Why not here?”

I shrugged. “Not sure. Maybe they’re just oddballs.”

Like me. Maybe that was why we got along. None of them were heavily involved with their guilds. Barely involved, in fact. Members in name only, for the most part. I knew they went to the required meetings, but they preferred to live on their own in the flats over the kebab place.

I started toward the gate, walking quickly through

the tunnel to the other side. I'd been here a week, and it was already starting to feel like home.

I appeared on the other side, standing in the dim corridor at the back of the Haunted Hound. The Devil appeared next to me, and we strode out into the pub.

The early crowd was here, a motley collection of strange supernaturals who liked to gather for tea and the paper first thing in the morning.

Quinn manned the bar. The handsome, muscular shifter looked at us, his eyes narrowing on the Devil.

"It's fine, Quinn." I knew he didn't like the Devil. Didn't trust him.

Neither did I.

"Sure." Quinn smiled coldly at the Devil, and the Devil smiled even more coldly back.

I didn't know what the issue was between them, and I didn't want to know.

"Are Mac and Eve here yet?" I took a seat at the bar.

"Not yet." He turned to me, his scowl transforming into a smile. "What can I get you?"

"Tea, please. And anything you've got for breakfast."

He nodded and didn't ask the Devil what he wanted, but he did bring him the same tea he served me. I'd taken my first sip when I heard Mac's voice from the other side of the room: "Carrow!"

I turned to look.

She and Eve approached. The strange black raven flew behind Eve. I watched the bird approach. The creature's eyes glinted. It looked strangely familiar. I shook the thought away and turned to Eve and Mac.

Eve's hair was bright white. When I'd first met her, it had been purple. She used magic to change it from day to day. Eve was a strange Fae, I'd learned. She made potions to sell, generally the province of the witches, not the Fae, and kept mostly to herself. Except for the raven, which she claimed not to see.

Mac gave the Devil a long look as she went around to the other side of the bar to stand near Quinn. Eve took a seat next to me, setting a pile of books down on the bar. The raven sat next to her, but she didn't so much as spare it a glance.

Quickly, I filled them in on everything we'd learned, starting at La Papillon and ending with my vision of the symbol at the hotel.

"When Carrow sent me the picture of the symbol, I knew I'd seen it somewhere." Eve flipped open one of the books and pointed to a symbol drawn there. "This is a compendium of sorcerer history, and this symbol is the mark of Mariketta the Vengeful."

"What did she want vengeance for?" I asked.

"Sorcerers are extremely loyal to their kind. And very intelligent. Someone sought to harness Mariketta's genius by compelling her to work for them." Eve looked toward the Devil. "Not the same way you do, though. They kidnapped her daughter, hoping to force Mariketta to do their bidding."

"I assume she refused?" I asked.

Eve nodded. "Exactly. She found where they were keeping the child, a heavily protected fortress hidden within Paris."

"Like Guild City?"

"Yes. Right among humans. But it was a single building, not a town like ours. Anyway, Mariketta used her magic to get her child back. They were no match for her, which they hadn't fully anticipated. After she left the fortress with her daughter, she enacted her vengeance." Eve's eyes glinted with a bit of bloodlust. "She left behind a device that blew up half of the fortress. But that wasn't the serious bit."

"There's something more serious than blowing up half their place and killing a bunch of them?" Mac asked.

"Oh, yes. The explosion destroyed the magic that hid their fortress from Paris. Those that survived were left with the bodies of their compatriots in full view of the human citizens. Their home was destroyed, their cover blown, and many of them were caught."

"What happened to them?" I couldn't imagine humans suddenly seeing magical beings like the ones I saw every day in Guild City. When I'd first walked into this pub, I'd thought a cosplay convention was happening. There had been no cosplay hundreds of years ago, but there had been a hell of a lot of suspicion of magic.

"The more powerful ones escaped," Eve said. "The

less powerful were burned at the stake as witches. It started one of the greatest witch hunts in Europe."

"Then that's what they plan to do here," the Devil said. "They'll blow up Black Church, the ceremonial center of our power. They want to recreate Mariketta's spell and reveal Guild City to the world."

"To humans." I cringed. "They're seeking Mariketta's crypt. Or they were. Which means they didn't have the spell when they first broke into your office," I told him.

"Do you know where the crypt is?" he asked Eve.

She nodded. "She's said to be buried at the Church on the Hill."

"The haunted one?" Mac asked.

"Haunted like this pub?" I looked toward the ghostly dog who slept in front of the fire.

"No." Mac shook her head. "Haunted in the bad way."

"It might even be Mariketta's magic that haunts it," Eve said. "People don't go there anymore. It's too dangerous."

"I'm not sure we have a choice." I frowned up at the Devil. "What about the key that the bartender saw Ivan give to the man who broke into your office?"

"We thought he was supposed to be a distraction, but maybe he accomplished more than that," the Devil said.

"Do you think he handed the key off to someone?"

"It's possible. He may have been working with a team, and he was the liaison with Ivan."

"But we don't know where this key is, right?" Mac asked.

I shook my head. "We don't."

"There were some witnesses on the human side who said that they saw the man approaching the gate," the Devil said.

"Humans?" Mac sounded aghast.

"No. Supernaturals who live near my gate. I pay them to keep an eye out."

"One of them might have seen something," said Quinn. "And perhaps they don't realize."

Mac nodded, a thoughtful gleam in her eye. "Tell you what…while you go to the Church on the Hill, I'll go talk to those people and see what my seer power tells me. Maybe they saw something that didn't stand out but was important. With any luck, I might get a clue and be able to trace his steps backward. Maybe we can still find that key."

"I like that plan." It seemed less dangerous for Mac, and we needed to find the damned key.

~

The Devil

. . .

Carrow and I left the Haunted Hound ten minutes later. Her three friends had come up with a plan to search for the missing key, and we were headed to the Church on the Hill.

In silence, we returned to Guild City. It was an overcast day when we appeared on the other side of the magical barrier, but the faint light suited Carrow. She seemed to glow despite it.

"Where is this church?" she asked.

"The edge of town, on the hill."

Her gaze moved in the direction I'd indicated. You couldn't see the church from here, not with the way the land rose, but the changing geography was obvious.

"How is there a hill in the middle of London?"

"Magic."

Her eyes narrowed on me. "Is it true you built this place when you left Transylvania?"

"I'm one man. I can't build a city." That part was the truth. But she wasn't wrong, either. I'd played a role in creating Guild City in the image of the walled cities of my homeland. But now wasn't the time to talk about it. "Come."

She grumbled but followed. I had the distinct impression I wasn't off the hook, that she was biding her time.

I'd seen Carrow when she really wanted answers. There was no hiding from her.

We strode across the city, and I was more aware than

ever of people crossing the street to avoid me. My reputation had come in exceedingly handy over the years, but now...

I glanced at Carrow and wondered what she thought.

There was enough humanity left in me that I knew it was odd to be feared. Not desirable when trying to convince someone you weren't the devil incarnate.

Despite my name.

"Call me Grey." The words left my lips before I'd even processed them.

She whipped her head around to stare at me. We were passing a shop that sold potions of some kind, and they were exploding in the window behind her. The clouds of gold and silver dust emphasized the look of surprise on her face.

"Really?" she asked.

I nodded. "It is my name, after all."

"Um...okay. Maybe."

Discomfort prickled against my neck. I turned back to the street and resisted rubbing my chest. It felt strange.

This *all* felt strange.

Fortunately, we reached the edge of town a moment later. Thank fates—a distraction from my idiocy.

The hill rose steeply here, small buildings crawling up the sides. They were primarily residential, though it wasn't the nicer part of town.

"Who lives here?" Carrow asked.

"Generally dark magic practitioners."

"Evil magic?"

"Normally, yes. Depending on how you use it."

"The Council allows them to stay here?"

"If they pay the right dues."

"Through you?"

I shook my head. "I don't tend to deal in dark magic. There's enough money to be made on the sidelines of light."

She gave me a considering look, and a strong desire for her approval flowed through me. I shook my head to drive off the feeling and turned back to the covered stairs that stretched up the hill. The rickety wooden steps were covered by a dilapidated peaked wooden roof that protected them from the rain.

Carrow stepped closer and peered up the stairwell, which extended more than a hundred meters upward. The space was narrow and dark, with shafts of light shining through the sides and the holes in the ceiling.

She whistled low. "Must take a lot of magic to hide a hill like this in London."

"An immense amount." I'd helped collect much of it when the city was founded. "There's a series of magical batteries that help power the spell that hides us."

She turned to me, her brows raised. "Magical batteries?"

I nodded. "Certain objects possess more magic than

others, either because of their history or what they are. They can be difficult to find, but the power in them can be used for many things."

"Could your enemies be threatening those?"

"Possibly. They're so well protected and hidden that I doubt they could find one. But it's always possible. If they are planning to blow up Black Church, I don't know how one would play a role in that."

She shivered, then began to climb the wooden stairs. I followed right behind her. Light streamed through the darkness, and as we climbed, it grew colder and colder.

She looked over her shoulder. "Is this the haunting?"

"Yes."

Snow began to fall outside, totally out of place in London at this time of year. She shivered hard and hugged her arms to her chest.

I stripped off my jacket and handed it to her.

She gave me a confused look.

"Put it on." Protectiveness itched under my skin, an uncomfortably unfamiliar feeling that I couldn't resist.

"No, thanks."

"You're not built for this cold. Put it on."

"Neither are you."

"Of course I am. I was born in the mountains of Transylvania." I scowled at her. "Besides, your shivering is distracting me."

"Fine." She tugged the jacket on, and satisfaction surged. "Thank you."

We hurried up the steps, pushing our way through the cold wind that whipped snow across our cheeks. A shiver rippled over my skin, but I ignored it. As we neared the top, the prickle of dark magic grew stronger.

"Ugh, that feels awful," Carrow said.

"Dark magic protections. Be alert."

The light at the top of the staircase beckoned, and we stepped out into the pale, watery sunlight of an overcast day. The snow stopped abruptly, and the simple church rose tall in front of us. White plaster covered the outside, and the windows gleamed in the light.

"We're at the back side. We need to get around to the front." I eyed the graveyard that surrounded it. "Keep an eye on the stones."

She shot a wary glance at them, then moved toward the church. We stayed close to the wall as we walked, but our presence seemed to irritate something. Faint magic vibrated on the air, prickling and sharp.

There was an eerie howl from the cemetery, and Carrow edged closer to my side. It was on the tip of my tongue to tell her not to worry—that I would protect her.

I bit it back.

It was true. I *would* protect her.

But she wouldn't want to hear it.

And it was...unlike me. We didn't have that kind of relationship.

The earth beneath the gravestones shifted, dirt

tumbling over rocks. The scent of death wafted toward us.

"Move quickly." I picked up the pace, and we ran for the door.

The grass over the gravestones broke apart, dirt rising through the cracks.

Bodies would come next.

I raised a hand, and magic surfaced and flowed through me. I directed it toward the bodies in the graves.

Stay down.

It was hard work—nearly impossible—but nothing rose as we hurried toward the church. Finally, the large doors loomed in front of us. I kept my magic flowing as I pulled one open, ushering her inside.

Carrow sprinted in and spun around to peer out. I darted in after her, looking behind to check the graveyard.

The dirt lay still. Nothing had risen, thank fates.

"The protective spell has died now that we've entered the church." I shut the door behind us. "At least, the spell on the graveyard."

"Were there really zombies back there?" Carrow stripped out of my jacket and handed it to me.

I took it. "I believe so. Something was trying to rise out there."

"And you stopped them with your magic? How?"

"I can compel people to tell me things—but it is their mind I am controlling, not their bodies. Their will is often too strong for me to do that. But the dead…"

"Easier?"

I nodded. "I couldn't make them tap dance, but that worked."

"Thank God, because I have no interest in meeting a zombie." She turned to look inside the church.

I followed her, my footsteps ringing in the silence. It was a quiet, simple space. The arched ceiling was plain and white. Dust covered the pews and altars, and the frescoes on the walls were faded and dim. The place echoed with silent emptiness.

I stepped farther into the church, searching for a clue. It had been centuries since I'd been here, and I'd never had reason to explore. "Now, where is our crypt?"

Together, we searched the interior perimeter of the small church. There were no doors that led underground. It was like our quarry had disappeared into thin air.

"Were they really ever here?" Carrow asked. "Or did we beat them? Because nothing looks disturbed."

"The entrance to the crypts could be around the outside."

Carrow shuddered. "I don't want to spend too much time out there unless we have to."

"Agreed." I strode up to one of the frescoes, which depicted a service in the church. It was strange for wall paintings like this to show scenes from the church within which they were placed, but the Church on the Hill was anything but normal.

"Look at this." I pointed to the painting, which seemed to show figures descending stairs in the floor.

"They're at the front of the altar." Carrow hurried toward the dusty platform depicted in the painting, and I followed.

There, perfectly inset into the floor, was a door, unnoticeable until we were standing on top of it.

Pleasure surged through me. This was unexpected, and surprises were rare for a vampire of my age.

I knelt, running my hands over the hinges. The dust had been disturbed there, pressed to the side by the opening of the door. The hinges themselves were now shiny and clean. "They've come this way."

An iron handle was set into the wood. Carrow reached for it, twisting it up and out to pull. It didn't budge. "It's locked."

"They didn't break through."

She studied the lock. "This is too big for the key that I saw in my vision. That was much smaller than this lock. Do you think they had another key?"

I shook my head. "Perhaps. But the priest who worked here before the church shut for good was an Englishman. I've no idea how one of his keys might have got into their hands, but it's possible. Maybe they used a spell to trick the door into opening."

"You knew the priest?"

I nodded and stood. "I also know where he kept important things like keys."

"How do you know that?" She rose to join me.

"I would visit here centuries ago." I looked down at the crypt. "Though I never cared what they did with their dead, so I was unfamiliar with this."

"A religious vampire?"

"Hardly. I was building my empire."

"With a church?"

"Most definitely with a church. They've always possessed great power in communities, and Father Alderage was no different."

"And he helped you set up your criminal enterprise?"

I shrugged, feeling a strange hollowness inside me. "We were friends, I suppose. And there was plenty in it for him."

"Like money."

"Of course, money. And power." I strode toward the far corner of the church. "Come. His quarters were back here."

I found the small wooden door that I hadn't stepped through in centuries. It opened easily beneath my palms. The interior looked like it hadn't been touched in over three hundred years, with a thick layer of dust over the ornate wooden furniture.

"Wow." Carrow whistled. "I'd say the maid is overdue."

I chuckled as I strode around the desk and chair to the stone wall behind. There, I knelt, reaching for the false stone, and slipped it out. An ancient iron keyring appeared, and I pulled it free.

As I stood and held it up, magic sparked in the air, prickly and fierce.

"What's that?" Carrow spun around, searching the room.

"Ghosts. And they don't like what we've just done."

11

CARROW

Cold fear pierced me. "Ghosts?"

The Devil—I tried to think of him as Grey, but it was hard—nodded, his brow set in a severe line. "They don't like that I've taken the key. Come on."

Quickly, he strode from the office. I followed, hurrying to keep up. The church itself was even colder, and figures drifted out from the walls, pale and transparent.

"Can they hurt us?" I stuck close to his side as we hurried toward the center of the church, where the altar still stood.

"Perhaps." He knelt, smoothly inserting the key.

I stood, spinning in a circle to keep an eye on the

ghosts that closed in on us. My heartbeat thundered in my ears as they neared. Each was dressed in an outfit that was at least three centuries out of date, but the malice on their faces was timeless.

The crystal at my throat glowed with heat, and I closed my fingers around it. The ghosts' eyes followed my movements.

"They want Orion's Heart." I clutched it tighter.

"It's powerful. They may think it can bring them back to life."

"Hell, no." I glared at the ghosts. "Back off."

"They won't listen." The jingle of the iron keys continued as he worked.

"Hurry up!" They were almost to me, so cold that I felt like my bones were chattering. "I don't know how to fight a ghost."

"You can't."

At the edge of the room, Cordelia appeared. The little raccoon raced toward me, holding her bushy tail high. She positioned herself between me and the ghosts, hissing wildly.

They cringed back.

"They don't like familiars," the Devil said.

As the key *snick*ed in the lock behind me, one of the ghosts got up its courage and lunged close.

"Beware your fated mate," it hissed.

I frowned. "What?"

"Come." The Devil stood and gripped my waist,

moving me forcibly toward the stairs that disappeared into the dark.

Cordelia maintained her position, teeth bared at the specters.

I gave them one last look as I hurried down the stairs, the Devil behind me. Had he heard the ghost?

He gave no indication.

Cool darkness enveloped me as we descended. Deep below the church, the air was silent and still. The ghosts stayed above, driven back by Cordelia, no doubt. Finally, I reached the bottom—a narrow hallway with a dirt floor.

It was nearly pitch black, and the Devil drew a lighter from his pocket. He flipped it on and lit the torch on the wall.

Golden light illuminated the long hallway, highlighting the tiny doors set into the walls on both sides. Each door was roughly one square meter in size, just big enough to fit a coffin. They were stacked six high and stretched endlessly down the hall.

There had to be dozens. Hundreds, even.

"Each of these must contain a body." I ran my fingertips over one, feeling a prickle of magic.

"You said you saw a symbol on one?"

"Yes. It's hers." I walked down the hallway, searching the little stone doors. Each was marked with a different name or symbol, but none were the one I sought.

Finally, at the end, we found an empty hole in the

grid of doors located roughly at chest level. The interior was so dark that it was impossible to see inside, but prickling magic spilled out.

A shiver raced over me. "The door is gone."

"Down there." The Devil crouched, running his hand over a slab of rock that lay on the ground. "They aren't hinged, so when the crypt is open, the door must be left on the ground."

I looked down and spotted the sorceress Mariketta's symbol. "They've beaten us here."

The Devil stood, slowly reaching toward the interior of the small crypt.

I leaned closer, trying to peer into the darkness. "Can you see anything? A body?"

He drew a small charm from his pocket and flicked his wrist. The stone began to glow a bright gold color that shed light inside the small space.

Shock lanced me. "It goes back forever."

"A tunnel." The Devil grinned.

"Why do you look so happy?" Nerves chilled my skin. "Do you have ulterior motives?"

"If I did, I wouldn't say so." He shook his head. "But no, I don't. I just like when the unexpected happens here in Guild City."

"Like the door in front of the altar."

"Yes. Immortality is a long time, and boredom is my enemy." He looked down at me, impossibly handsome, his eyes gleaming with interest. "Ready to explore?"

I nodded. "Can you give me a boost?"

"Yes." He stored the glowing gem back in his pocket and gripped my waist in his strong hands. A shiver raced through me, and he hoisted me up.

I crawled into the tunnel, then tumbled forward into a much larger space. It was tall enough that I could stand, a strange trick of magic. I rose slowly and stepped out of the Devil's way.

He climbed up to join me, and we stood side by side in the tunnel. It was a tight fit, close enough that I could feel his warmth and smell the fresh scent of his soap as I pressed myself back against the wall.

"I'll lead." He pulled his glowing charm from his pocket to light the way and started down the tunnel.

I followed, sticking close behind him, glad to let him face whatever monsters might lurk in the dark. The path descended deep underground, sloping downward sharply.

"We must be going back into town," I said, my innate sense of direction kicking in.

"I had no idea." He sounded thrilled.

"You aren't worried?"

"I'm not as familiar with fear as I once was." There was a hint of deception to his voice, and I wondered why.

"That's not true."

He looked over his shoulder at me, his face cast mostly in shadow. "Last night, I feared for you."

"Oh." That was *not* what I'd been expecting.

Cursed Mate.

Did he have feelings for me? Was that the *mate* part of the equation? But what about the cursed part?

He turned back and continued, going deeper and deeper until we had to be underneath the city itself. There were no other tunnels leading off the main one, and the narrow darkness was starting to press in on me. I kept my eyes glued on the light.

"There are many tunnels beneath Guild City," he said. "Most are managed by the Dwarves. This one must be deeper to avoid intersecting."

"Wow."

Ahead, the Devil slowed. "Something happened here."

I edged up behind him and peered over his shoulder. Spikes protruded from the walls, their tips stained dark red. I recoiled. "That's blood."

"Fresh blood."

I looked again. The spikes protruded from each wall, hundreds of them, their tips touching. There were bits of fabric hanging from some of them where they'd torn at a person's clothing. There were so many of them that they formed an impassable wall.

The Devil reached out and snapped one off.

"What are they made of?" I asked.

"Iron."

He broke another, then another, creating a passage

for us. Soon, it was completely open. I followed him through, reaching up for one of the taller ones to see if it really was iron.

It didn't budge beneath my hands.

He shot me a grin over his shoulder. "Didn't trust me?"

"I do now."

He turned back, then faltered.

I stopped, mimicking his motions.

"One of them didn't make it."

Looking past him, I found a body sprawled in the hall. Blood pooled around it from the wounds. He'd gotten away from the spikes, but not soon enough.

"Let me." I skirted the Devil and knelt by the dead man, keeping my gaze averted from the worst of the wounds. I searched his clothes and the area around him, finding nothing.

I laid my hand on him, trying to force myself to find something useful.

What are you planning?

Bits of information flashed through my head, but the only thing I could find was the explosion I'd already seen.

"Are you getting anything?"

"Nothing new." I needed more practice.

"Come on. We need to hurry. There's got to be more than just him."

I nodded and stood, stepping over the body and

following the Devil farther down the hall. We wound through the tunnel for what felt like days.

The Devil slowed. "We're nearing something. Can you feel it?"

"The magic is changing, isn't it?" The way it vibrated over my skin was different. And the glow was faintly green.

"It is." I heard the frown in his voice. "Feels like sorcerer magic."

"Makes sense, since Mariketta was a sorceress. But why the hell is there a tunnel?"

"It terminates ahead." He stopped.

I squeezed up beside him. The air gleamed with an oily green light. "What is that?"

"A portal. Unlike any I've ever seen."

"Do we go inside?"

He nodded. "I think we must."

Excitement and dread warred within me, but I had no choice.

I stepped forward, determined to get it over with. The Devil's hand closed over my arm, stopping me.

"I'll go first." His tone demanded no argument, and he stepped around me. "If something goes wrong, get out of here."

He stepped through, disappearing.

I waited briefly. How was I supposed to recognize if something went wrong?

Everything *seemed* okay.

I hurried after him, letting the ether suck me in and spin me through space. Anxiety made my stomach pitch even harder. Where the hell were we going?

Portals were one thing, but portals to entirely unknown places were another matter entirely.

The magic spat me out into bright, humid warmth. I blinked, the sun blinding me. As my vision slowly clearly, my ears picked up the sounds of birds and the crash of waves. The scent of the sea rushed over me, and the warmth made my soul come alive.

Heaven.

The scene that unrolled in front of me was divine.

We stood on a sandy beach overlooking a crystal blue sea. Green mountains towered behind us, and white gulls swooped on the wind, cawing in the air. A pale white structure was built on the sand. The marble folly was round, with pillars supporting a domed roof.

Something flashed out of the corner of my vision, and I looked left, spotting what looked like a section of gray stone wall.

That was odd.

The Devil stood near me, studying the scene. A woman stood within the folly, leaning against a pillar and staring out to sea.

It took my head a moment to clear. The sheer beauty of this place had stolen my wits. But we'd just been in a crypt, and now we were in this divine place.

"Are we in heaven?" I asked.

Again, there was a flash of something that looked like a stone wall on the other side of this heavenly scene.

The Devil shook his head. "No. This isn't an afterworld." He frowned. "Something is different."

"Afterworld? Like the afterlife?" Fear chilled me. "We aren't *dead*, right?"

This place was gorgeous, but I didn't want to stay here alone forever with the Devil—no matter how sexy he was—and a crazed sorceress named Mariketta.

"We are not dead." His gaze met mine, calming. "You can feel your heartbeat, can you not?"

I nodded. "Yeah. Yeah."

The woman turned to us, her dark hair and white dress blowing in the wind. The gown was simple and loose, the perfect beach dress for a goddess on vacation. Mariketta was no goddess—to my knowledge, at least—but she looked like one.

She was impossibly beautiful as she strolled toward us. "More visitors?"

Her voice rang like birdsong, and laughter followed it.

Childlike laughter.

I frowned. That wasn't Mariketta.

I looked behind her and saw a child splashing in the sea.

The daughter she'd saved, and then avenged.

I looked back to her and slowly approached, the Devil a pace behind me. He'd made a point to charge into danger first, and I wondered if he were playing it safe now to avoid frightening Mariketta.

Hearing what she'd done to that town in France made me think she didn't need coddling, however.

Behind her, I once again saw the flicker of stone wall.

"I am Carrow Burton." I gestured to my companion. "And this is the Devil of Darkvale."

Mariketta leaned against one of the white pillars. "How kind of you to pay me a visit. It gets rather dull here, despite its beauty."

"What is this place?" I asked, unable to help myself.

"The Sorcerers' Guild tower, of course. There are reasons we never let anyone inside unescorted."

"But you're telling us about it?" Worry pricked.

She shrugged and laughed. "Who will you tell?"

"My friends?"

"If you make it out of here."

Aaand there it was. My senses had already been on high alert, but now they were laser focused. "Are you not dead, then?"

She laughed, a lovely sound despite the slight aura of dark magic that surrounded her. I didn't get the impression that she was explicitly evil. Not even close, really. But she would do what it took to get what she wanted, and her magic made that clear.

"Oh, I'm quite dead. But sorcerers do things on their own schedule. If we choose, we can each have an enchanted room in the guild tower until we want to cross over."

"Why have you not crossed over?" Did it have something to do with the tragedy we were trying to prevent? Could she help us?

Mariketta gestured to the child playing in the surf. "She is not yet ready." She shrugged. "And this is a lovely place to spend time."

"You mentioned other visitors," I said. "Did they take something?"

"Indeed, they did." She gestured us forward. "But first, drinks."

I shot the Devil a look. Did we have time for this?

He nodded slightly. We didn't have much choice. I had no idea if his magic could compel her to tell us what we wanted, so we'd have to convince her.

She led us to wooden lounge chairs at the edge of the folly. They faced the crashing waves and playing child. She waved her hand, and tropical orange and red drinks appeared on the tables next to us. A happy buzz floated through me at the sight of them.

"Have a Hawaiian Sunset," she said. "They're lovely."

The Devil hesitated. He looked at them, as though trying to decipher their ingredients.

Mariketta laughed. "I promise they are not poisonous."

We sat on the lounge chairs. Grey looked entirely out of place. Instead of reclining, he sat on the side, his arms propped on his knees as he watched Mariketta with keen eyes. He was a man who hadn't relaxed in centuries, and it was obvious.

Me, on the other hand...I could get used to this.

I sipped the drink gingerly, to be polite. Fruity sweetness exploded on my tongue. It tasted divine. I wanted to gulp it but resisted.

Still, I felt great. This place was amazing. "You should sell tickets."

She laughed. "That would defeat the point."

"Why is this place connected to your crypt?" the Devil asked. "It seems like a security hazard."

"We need the grave magic in the church's crypt to help fuel this place, and the tunnel facilitates that." She scowled. "As for the ones who broke in, they shouldn't have been able to. But they were powerful."

"Do you know what they intend to do?" I asked.

"Destroy Guild City." There was an unmistakable scowl in her voice.

"That includes this place." I frowned. "If it's fueled by magic from the Sorcerers' Guild Tower and the holy ground of the church, it will disappear when those places are destroyed."

Mariketta rubbed her arms, a worried look rushing over her face. "Indeed."

"Then why are we drinking and having a chat?" I sat upright, my head clearing briefly. I looked down at the beverage. "What was in this?"

"Truth serum." Her eyes flicked to ours, hard and clear. "It gave you a buzz but was harmless. I need to know who you truly are if I am going to help you."

She wasn't just inviting us to a lovely cocktail party.

Of course she wasn't.

"The Devil knew that." She nodded at him, and I looked over, finding half his glass gone.

"Of course." His voice was smooth as he gestured to the drink. "And you can see we're willing to comply. We want to save Guild City, and with it, your place here."

She nodded, appearing satisfied by our truths. "I tried to keep them from taking what they wanted. They shouldn't have been able to make it into this place, but somehow, they managed."

"What did they take?"

"Memories," she said. "*My* memories."

"Of the spell that you used to get vengeance for your daughter?" My gaze moved to the young girl who still splashed in the surf.

"Exactly. It was the only place that my spell was hidden."

"How do we stop them?"

"The secret is in the spell," she said.

"That's vague." I frowned. "Have you not warned the other sorcerers? Couldn't they stop this?"

"Warn them how? I cannot leave this room, and the magic in this place weakens every time someone enters. They do not visit unless there are intruders."

Behind her, I caught sight of a brief glimpse of the stone wall through the image of the ocean. The magic here *was* weakening.

"The sorcerers will be coming?" I stiffened and looked at the Devil. They would not like finding us here, that was certain.

"Yes. Soon enough, I imagine."

"Then we'll tell them what we know."

"They'll strike first and ask questions later." She shrugged. "You are intruders, after all."

12

The Devil

Damn it, the sorceress was right. We probably wouldn't have time to explain why we were here. This guild hated me, and they were notorious for protecting their space with violence.

I leaned forward. "Tell us how to stop Ivan. Please."

She nodded. "First, you must vow that you will repair the door to my crypt and remove my symbol from the stone. I do not want anyone else paying me a visit. My protections were clearly not enough."

"I vow it."

The Sorceress looked toward Carrow, her eyebrows raised.

"I vow it as well," Carrow said.

"Good. You have the ability to read people and things?"

"Yes, but I can't control it well."

"Try anyway." Mariketta held out her hand.

"All right." Carrow leaned closer, resting her fingertips against the top of Mariketta's hand.

Her magic flared, strong and bright. The scent of lavender overpowered the seaside aroma of the room, and the taste of oranges exploded on my tongue.

Mariketta's eyes widened. "Your signature is quite something."

"I know. I need to get control of it."

"Indeed, you do. Unless things have changed drastically, the Council will not stand for it."

"Things haven't changed." Carrow's eyes shut, and she drew in a deep breath.

Her signature grew even stronger, and I frowned.

Mariketta met my gaze, and I could see my thoughts reflected in her eyes.

Carrow's magic was changing—growing. I sensed it. This was highly unusual.

We'd have to hide it from the Council somehow.

Minutes passed, and I shifted. This was taking too long. The air seemed to grow restless, the tower seeming to come alive.

"They know you're here," Mariketta said. "That's what you are feeling. They're coming."

Carrow's eyes popped open. "The sorcerers?"

"Yes. They've sensed the disturbance. But the tower is enormous on the inside. It will take them a moment to reach this place. Did you get what you need?"

"A spell, yes." Concern echoed in Carrow's voice. "I have the words in my head. But I don't know what to do with it. If I say it, will it stop Ivan?"

"You don't know how to stop it?" I asked.

Carrow shook her head.

"You'll know when the time comes." Mariketta leaned forward and tapped the crystal that hung around Carrow's neck. "And you have all that you need."

"Wait, what do you mean?" Carrow frowned.

A shout sounded from the other side of the walls that wavered through the tropical scenery, carrying over the sound of the waves.

I stood. "We must go."

"Please." Carrow turned to Mariketta. "I don't feel prepared. Tell us anything helpful. Anything."

"You must go *under* to reach them. Not through. *Under.*"

"What?" Confusion flickered in her gaze. "I don't understand."

"You will. And don't forget...you'll only make it past the barrier at dusk. Make it into the church, and you have everything you need to stop them."

"That's still unclear." Frustration echoed in Carrow's voice.

"It will become so." Mariketta voice rang with conviction.

I spun in a circle, searching for the door. The sorcerers were getting closer. "How do we get out of here?"

"There's only one exit," Mariketta said. "And they're going to come through it."

Shite. "We'll have to fight our way past."

"Tell them we're here to help," Carrow said.

"I'll try, but..."

"Carrow, come here." I needed to be able to protect her. "Mariketta, where is the door?" The beautiful scenery flickered, revealing the stone wall beyond, but no door.

"I don't know. This space is always changing. The room itself is unknown to me." Mariketta moved toward her daughter. "Best of luck to you.'

"Tell them we're here to help," Carrow repeated.

An explosion sounded from behind me, and I spun. A man burst through the door, his dark cape flowing around him. His brow lowered over his eyes. "You."

He *hated* me, and so did the rest of them.

"We're here to—" Carrow began.

The sorcerer threw a fireball. She dove left, narrowly avoiding a hit.

I lunged for the guard. Raising my hand, I flung my magic at him. "Do not attack us."

His mouth snapped shut, and fire blazed in his eyes. He raised his hand, his palm glowing with red light.

"Do *not.*" I forced him to comply, shooting Carrow a look. "Get out of here. I can't hold him for long."

"They're here to help, Mauritius," Mariketta said.

Mauritius didn't spare her a glance. He didn't want to hear her. He was enraged by my presence in their tower. *No one* invaded the sorcerers' space without consequences.

Carrow raced for the door. Mauritius struggled against my hold as Carrow slipped around him.

I looked at Mariketta. "Thank you. I will mend your crypt. When he's calm, I'd appreciate it if you explained things to him."

She shrugged. "I will try."

I nodded and hurried after Carrow, not letting go of my hold on Mauritius. He growled as I went by, and I prayed that Mariketta could talk some sense into him. We might need help taking down Ivan.

The hall outside of Mariketta's enchanted room was long and dark. The stone floor and walls blended, and the air glowed with a faint gray light that seemed to have no source.

I heard footsteps to our right.

"Which way?" Carrow looked frantically in either direction. "I can hear them coming, but I can't tell where they are."

"Go left."

She sprinted down the hall, and I followed, covering her back. It seemed endless, impossibly long for a tower at the edge of Guild City.

Up ahead, another hallway intersected with ours. Footsteps pounded toward us.

"Look out ahead!" I said.

Carrow slowed. Two sorcerers sprinted out of the darkness, a man and a woman in cloaks, their eyes flashing with anger.

The woman raised her hand. Crimson light glowed from her palm, matching her red hair. She hurled it at us.

We dove out of the way, skidding on the stone ground.

The male sorcerer hurled another blast. It struck me in the leg, and pain flared. I forced it back, calling upon the strength and power I'd harnessed over the long centuries.

I surged upright and launched myself at them. Grabbing them by the lapels, I smashed their heads together. They dropped to the ground, unconscious.

"Are they dead?" Carrow asked.

"No." I'd pulled my punches to avoid it, though I could have crushed their skulls if I'd wanted. Hopefully, they'd realize that when they woke and not create too much trouble. "Let's go."

We sprinted around them, heading farther down the hall.

"We need to find stairs to the roof," I said. "We'll never make it through the main part of their tower."

Magic surged around us. The sorcerers were gearing up for battle, searching the halls for us, ready to strike. We couldn't run into anymore.

"Stairs!" Carrow pointed ahead, and I spotted them.

A narrow stairwell diverged off the hall.

We raced toward it and stopped in front of the entrance, panting. The darkened stairwell stretched up and down. Carrow headed up.

I followed. She stopped abruptly, and I slammed into her, grabbing her waist as she stumbled forward. "What is it?"

"This doesn't go up."

"Yes, it does."

"It doesn't." She turned with a frown. "I can feel it. We need to go down if we want to reach the roof."

"Are you sure?"

"I've always had a great sense of direction. Eerily so. I'm right, I know it."

"Let's go, then."

Side by side, we raced along the wide stairwell.

The stairs shifted and headed up instead of down.

"Sorcerers." I shook my head. "Tricky bastards."

We sprinted up flight after flight, passing several other hallways on different levels. Two of them were empty, but the third...

We passed it, and a surge of magic prickled the air. I

turned back as a sorcerer lunged out of the hallway behind us. Cloak whipping in the darkness, he raised a hand that gleamed with sparkling green and gold magic.

My heartbeat thundered. This was a killing blow, a deadly variety of sorcerer magic impossible to mistake and one powerful enough to kill even me.

The sorcerer hurled it at us with an evil sneer.

The green vortex of magic expanded, filling the stairwell. I threw myself in front of Carrow, blocking her from the assault.

The magic plowed into me, blinding me. Agony exploded throughout my body, sending my organs into a meat grinder.

I stumbled and collapsed on the stairs.

Carrow

Green magic exploded around us, and I staggered and went to my knees. Behind me, the Devil cried out in pain.

I scrambled to my feet and spotted him below me on the stairs. He was unconscious. He'd taken that blow to protect me.

Dead?

Fear spiked.

The sorcerer raised his hand again, a vengeful gleam in his eyes. The magic that sparked around his palm was faint. Was he recharging?

I didn't know much about magic, but I prayed that was true. I couldn't survive the kind of blast that had hit the Devil.

I rushed the sorcerer, leaping over the Devil and hurtling down the stairs like a train. As I plowed into him, he crashed onto his back, breaking my fall with his body. Struggling to rise, he struck me with his palm, and pain blossomed as his magic slammed into me. My vision blackened, and my organs trembled in shock.

Blindly, I raised my fist and punched him on the chin. His head snapped to the side, and I blinked, my vision returning. I'd taken a partially charged blast, and it had almost wiped me out.

If he *fully* recharged, I'd be dead.

The sorcerer beneath me seemed dazed. I hit him again and he slumped, unconscious.

Heart pounding, I scrambled off him and up the stairs, crouching by the Devil's prone form. I gripped his big shoulders and shook them. "Wake up, Grey! Wake up!"

His eyes fluttered open, though his gaze seemed blurred. "You called me Grey."

"I...did." He'd taken a hit for me, and that had changed how I thought of him.

"What happened?" he asked.

"The sorcerer struck you with green magic. I don't know what kind of spell it was, but it looked bad."

"Killing blow." He groaned. Pushing himself upright, he staggered to his feet.

I joined him. Wrapping my arm around his waist, I helped him up the stairs. He gained strength with every step, but I could tell that the attack had taken a lot out of him.

"We're nearly there," I said, panting from the climb.

"You can sense it?"

"Wishful thinking." I pushed harder, climbing onward.

Finally, we reached the roof. The cold evening wind whipped across my cheeks as I searched for the stairs we'd taken before. The secret stairwell was located on the exterior of the building, hidden within the wall.

"There."

Grey stumbled forward, and I hurried to his side, offering my support to him. We found the secret stairwell and started down. At one point, we lost our footing and nearly rolled to the bottom. It almost would have been a relief. I'd never felt so weak and exhausted.

Finally, we reached the top of the wall that surrounded the city and tottered out.

Grey dug into his pocket and pulled out a transport charm, but he didn't throw it.

"Come on!" I said. "Let's get out of here."

"Need to get farther from their tower. A spell prevents us from transporting."

Together, we weaved along the wall and away from the tower. Suddenly, shouts sounded above us, and I looked up. Silhouetted against the moonlight, three sorcerers stood on the roof.

"Will they attack?" I asked.

"Probably not outside of their tower."

A blast of yellow magic hurtled down at us.

With the last of his strength, Grey shoved me aside and lunged in the opposite direction. The force of his blow sent me skidding out of harm's way as the blast plowed into the stone. The shock waves hit Grey, slamming him the wall.

"Those bastards." He heaved himself upright and lurched toward me. "They shouldn't be attacking outside their tower."

He held out his hand, and I took it. Quick as a snake, he hurled the transport charm to the ground. Silver smoke poofed upward, and we leapt inside.

The ether sucked us in and spun us around, spitting us out in front of his tower. He swayed, his strength flagging. The bouncers at the door hurried over, worry on their faces.

"What'd you do to him?" growled the one on the left. A lion shifter, from the look of his wild golden hair.

"Not...her fault." Grey went to his knees.

"The sorcerers hit him with something." I knelt beside Grey, worry twisting in my chest.

"Come on, boss." The lion shifter gripped Grey and hoisted him upright, nearly dragging him toward the door. "We'll get you the healer."

The other shifter opened the door for them, and I raced after them. Miranda darted from behind the desk and hurried up to Grey.

"What happened?" she asked, patting Grey's cheeks to rouse him.

"The sorcerers hit him with a huge blast of green and gold light," I said.

She gave me a fierce look. "A killing blow? You're serious?"

"Yes."

"Bastards. We'll have their heads for this. That's deadly magic." She looked at the guard who wasn't supporting Grey's big frame. "Fetch the healer. Immediately."

"Will he be okay?" I demanded.

"I don't know. If he weren't so strong, he'd be dead already."

"His immortality won't help him?"

"It makes him stronger, but he's not immune to trauma or powerful magic." She looked at the lion shifter who was holding Grey upright. "Take him to his quarters."

"Aye." The shifter helped Grey along, who stubbornly stayed on his feet.

When I started to follow, Miranda glared at me. "I'm coming," I insisted, my voice firm, and she nodded in assent.

We wound through the halls, rising several stories and reached a part of the tower that was new to me. Slowly, Grey raised his hand and pressed it to the huge wooden door. Magic sparked, and the door opened.

The lion shifter dragged him in. Miranda and I trailed after them, walking into a beautiful, though austere, living room with massive windows overlooking a moonlit sea. Waves crashed on the rocky shore.

I blinked in surprise. This couldn't be real. Not in London.

But it *looked* real.

"Magic," Miranda said, catching my shock.

We entered another room, a massive sleeping chamber decorated in the same spartan style. A huge window overlooked snow-covered mountains gleaming in the moonlight. Again, the scene was so real that I could swear I smelled the icy snow through the glass.

They helped Grey to the bed, and the vampire lay on it with a groan.

"What did the magic do to him?" I stared, gazing worriedly at him.

"Pulverized his organs." Miranda sounded pissed. "Watch over him. I'm going to go help find the healer."

Both she and the bouncer moved toward the door.

"Wait!" I followed them with my gaze. "Will he die?"

Miranda's jaw tightened, and she said nothing.

Yes.

That was what her silence meant. *Yes.*

I went to Grey and sat on the bed beside him. He lay on the dark sheets, his skin pale and cold. I reached for his hand, gripping tightly. My feelings were jumbled and confused.

He'd saved me.

He'd lied to me.

He might die.

"Grey." I squeezed his hand. "Wake up, Grey. You're fine."

The words were stupid. He clearly wasn't fine.

"Why did you push me out of the way?"

He said nothing, but the corner of his mouth perked up the tiniest little bit. I rested my hand on his heart, feeling the slow, soft thud. It was so weak.

Fear chilled my skin.

"Grey, you have to hold on."

But he wouldn't be able to. I could feel it even now, in the slowing of his heart. How long would it take Miranda to find the healer?

Not in time.

The terrifying thought blasted through me. She wouldn't find the healer in time. He would die.

Grief pierced my soul. I didn't want him to die. I

didn't know what he meant to me or how I really felt, but I *knew* I didn't want him to die.

The memory of his bite at Temple Church flashed in my mind. My blood had healed him then. It could heal him now.

It was worth a try.

My heart pounding violently, I leaned over him and pressed my neck to his mouth. "Drink, Grey."

He didn't move.

Fear pulsed through me.

I climbed on top of him, straddling his hard body so that my neck was better aligned with his mouth. I gripped his hair in one hand, lifted his head, and pressed his lips to my neck. "Bite me."

A low groan tore from his throat, and his lips parted. Despite their chill, they were soft and smooth against my skin. When his tongue swiped against my skin, heat blazed in its wake.

I shuddered, unable to help myself.

Grey's fangs sank into my flesh, slowly and precisely. Pleasure exploded through me, and every muscle in my body seemed to clench.

When he began to draw on my blood, I moaned.

He mirrored the noise, a groan escaping his throat. His strong hands gripped me, one at my waist and one at my head, holding me pinned against him. I felt like prey, but...

I liked it.

Ecstasy streaked through me as he fed, his tongue laving and soothing the faint burn of his bite. I moved against him, craving friction and heat.

As he drank, his strength returned. I could feel it in his grip, in the warmth of his skin and the pounding of his pulse. He rolled me over and pressed me down into the mattress with his weight.

Fear flared, briefly, but it gave my desire an edge. I reached up and sank my hands into his hair, clamping my legs around his waist. He moved against me, thrusting in a rhythm that made pleasure coil deep within me.

It tightened, threatening to take me over the edge.

Instead, a vision flashed in my mind: Grey, drinking me to the death.

Not now, but in the future. Sometime soon. Fear chased away the heat.

The bite that brought such pleasure would also bring my end.

13

Grey

The world had become a cocoon of lavender and heat. My head spun as Carrow's blood spilled over my tongue, hot and delicious.

She was pinned beneath me on the bed, writhing as her thighs gripped my hips. The heat and softness of her was such an incredible contrast to the cold austerity of my life.

I wanted to sink into her. To stay here forever.

I drew more deeply on her neck, grinding myself against her, wanting more of her soft whimpers in my ears.

When the cries became more frantic, a beast arose inside me. She began to struggle, trying to push me off her. For the briefest second, the monster inside me wanted to pin her harder, draw more firmly.

Sanity returned. Horrified, I heaved myself off of her.

No.

Disgust surged through me, sickening me, and I nearly vomited.

What had I done? What had I *nearly* done?

I leapt from the bed, putting distance between Carrow and me. Hazy memories flashed through my mind. I'd been partially conscious, but I remembered.

The beast within me had almost risen.

I turned away, unable to look at her with the memories still swirling in my head.

"Grey? Are you all right?"

"I'm—" I cleared my throat, wishing it were as easy to clear my head. "Fine."

I stalked to the window, past the grand piano that I no longer played, and stared out at the mountains. The Carpathians—my home. Full of bears and wolves and other monsters like myself.

I was better suited to that place.

I heard Carrow climb out of bed, and I drew in a deep breath, forcing myself under control. I turned to her, my gaze going to the bite marks at her neck. The wound was already closing, but her blood gleamed dark red in the moonlight.

"Are you better?" she asked.

I forced my mind to the present, away from the fear of what I had almost done to her.

Drink her to the death.

"Yes. Thank you." Gratitude welled within me, followed by awe. "You saved me."

"Anyone would."

"Hardly." I shook my head. "And it doesn't matter if they did. Not all blood can heal me like that."

"Really?"

"Only yours."

Shadows crossed her face, followed by fear. The memory of her struggling beneath me surged to the surface, and the queasiness returned. "Did I...force you?" I asked. The idea made me want to throw myself back into the sorcerers' tower and let them barrage me with killing blows until I was no more.

"No." She shook her head, eyes wide. "You didn't. Not until—"

"You started struggling." I leaned back against the window, nearly lightheaded.

"You stopped right away."

"I took too much."

"No...no, that's not it." She chewed on her lip. Her eyes were dark as they searched mine. "I didn't struggle because of what you were doing. I had a vision."

"A vision? I thought your power didn't work on me."

"Normally, it doesn't. But this...it was so powerful, I was forced to see it."

Her dark tone worried me. "What did you see, Carrow?"

"We're Cursed Mates."

"I've heard that."

"I didn't know what it means, but now I have an idea."

"And?" I clenched my fists.

"Sometime in the future, you will drink me to death."

"I would never."

"If you won't, then you will die."

"Then I die."

She blinked at me, surprise flickering briefly in her eyes. It was there and gone so quickly that I almost wasn't sure if I saw it. "You would, wouldn't you?"

"I've lived a long enough life." I wasn't keen to die. After centuries of immortality, the idea was almost absurd. But if the alternative was her death, it wasn't a question.

"You took the killing blow from the sorcerers for me," she said. "Why?"

"You really can't guess?"

"Um—"

I shrugged, not keen on elucidating. "Don't be too concerned with it."

She looked at me like I was insane. "You tried to sacrifice your life for mine, and I'm not supposed to be concerned with it?"

"We have bigger problems."

She scowled. "In the immediate future, yes. After that? This is the biggest one, as far as I can see."

Damned Cursed Mates. At least the name finally made sense. "It won't happen if we don't fall for each other."

I turned back to the window, unable to look at her anymore. My words were ridiculous, and if I'd had to look into her eyes while saying them, I'd never have got them out.

"Right." Her voice sounded odd, but I couldn't place it. "Good plan."

A knock sounded at the door. Miranda and the healer rushed inside.

Miranda pulled up short, her eyes widening. "Devil. You're...standing."

I nodded. "Thanks to Carrow."

Miranda's gaze flashed to Carrow. "But how? You're not a healer."

Carrow shrugged. "I've got the touch."

She didn't mention the bite, and I was glad. It was personal. As much as I liked Miranda, we didn't have that kind of relationship.

"Am I not needed?" The old healer frowned, his bushy brows drawing close over his pale green eyes. The white cloak he wore was a relic from an older age. But then, so was he.

"No, but thank you, Doratio."

The healer nodded and backed out of the room.

Miranda gazed at Carrow and me in confusion, but she swallowed her questions. "Can I bring you anything?"

"Dinner, please." I looked at Carrow. "Something in particular?"

"Um, no." She still looked faintly shell-shocked, and I couldn't blame her.

Miranda disappeared

"There's more to this Cursed Mate bond," I said to Carrow. "There must be. But we don't have time for it now."

"I agree," she said. "I like your plan. There's no reason we should…fall for each other."

I nodded and tried to keep my expression placid.

I'd spent so many years feeling nothing that it was easy to tell when I was going off the rails. I was well and truly gone over her. No question.

I shoved the thought to the back of my mind.

"For someone immortal, you sure almost die a lot." She tried to make it a joke, an attempt to change the tone of the room.

It didn't work, but I played along. "You're dangerous."

"True." Her gaze dropped to my shirt, and I realized that it was blackened and charred from the sorcerer's spell.

"Let me change clothes." I strode away from her,

desperate for a moment to myself. A moment to gather my wits and return to the coldness that kept me in control.

Carrow

Head reeling, I watched Grey walk toward a closet. As he neared it, he stripped his shirt off over his head and disappeared inside. I got the briefest glimpse of hard muscles and scarred flesh and had to turn away.

Shocked, I stared out the windows at the impossible view.

That vision had been real.

We truly were Cursed Mates. I'd seen no details—just the two scenes and a deep understanding of what was to come.

I thumped my head against the glass. "God, I wish I were a witch."

The witches had it so good. They created spells and potions and sold them for beer money while partying in their tower. None of this visions-of-the-future shit.

Seeing my own future was just too much.

Especially when it was deadly.

Shake it off, honey.

Cordelia's voice sounded from down below, and I

turned to look. She sat a few feet away in the shadow of the huge piano I hadn't even noticed. A massive wall of bookshelves sat behind her, stuffed to the brim with books. Another thing I hadn't noticed.

"How did you get in here?" I asked.

How do I get anywhere? And you need to knock that look off your face. Moaning doesn't become you.

"Do you know what I saw in my vision? What lies ahead of me?"

No. And I don't need to. You've got real problems staring at you now, so you've got to deal with them. Don't go borrowing trouble.

"Don't go borrowing trouble." I stared at her, liking that phrase. "You're right."

Of course I'm right.

Deep in my soul, I knew that I'd have to confront the vision I'd had, but not now. I needed to focus. We had twenty-four hours to save Guild City.

"Thanks, Cordelia."

She nodded. *You can owe me a kebab.*

"Sure." I made a shooing motion. "Now, you should scram. We don't need the Devil knowing you can get into his place."

She tapped her head with a little claw. *Good thinking.*

She disappeared, and I pulled out my mobile to call Mac.

My friend picked up on the third ring without bothering with hello. "You find anything good?"

"Yeah. Can you meet?"

"Not yet. Almost got some info, though."

"Really?"

"Yep. Tracking this one last guy. He's supposed to get off work in a couple hours, and we can nab him."

"Shall we meet in the morning, then?" That would give us a day to stop this thing. I'd rather get started right away, but we didn't have enough info. And I needed some rest. So did Grey. We'd be staggering to the fight at this rate.

"First thing, your place. Sound good?" Mac asked.

"Sounds good. And hey, be safe."

"Always."

We hung up, and I turned to see Grey enter the room. He'd put on a clean shirt, and his expression looked less stunned. He'd shown more emotion after that bite than I'd ever seen, and I wanted to get to the bottom of it.

As if he could see what I was thinking, he swiftly changed the subject. "You called Mac?"

"Yes. They're on the trail of something, which is good, since I only got the words of a spell and nothing else from Mariketta."

"We still don't know about the key or how they plan to do it."

"We should know in the morning if Mac is right."

He nodded.

A knock sounded at the door again, and Miranda

entered with two servers carrying massive trays. They set them on the table in the main living room and disappeared like ghosts.

"Go to the Sorcerers' Guild," Grey said to Miranda. "Try to convince them that we meant no harm and have them contact us."

She grimaced. "I'll do my best, but I'm not sure my charm is going to do any good there."

"Try. If anyone can do it, you can. And keep working on the various guilds. See if you can get the more reticent ones to evacuate their people from city."

"I will." She departed silently.

My stomach roared, and I went to the table, ravenous. It was laid with an enormous spread of incredible variety. Steak pie, curry, pasta, and even pasties with gleaming golden crust. Grey joined me, and we ate in silence, finishing quickly and efficiently.

When I'd downed the last bite of my fish and chips, he said, "Your magic is changing."

"I know." I thought of the way I'd been able to zoom in on the vision of Mariketta's crypt, and then of how I'd had a hard time getting the information I needed from her memories. My powers were totally unreliable. "But how do *you* know?"

"I can feel it." His jaw tightened. "And that's dangerous."

My shoulders slumped.

"It's one thing not to be able to control your magic,"

he said. "That's bad enough. But you have magic that is constantly growing and changing. *That* is unheard of."

"I can't let the Council know."

"You can't." A deep frown cut across his face. "I can control them to a point, but I can only do so much. I can't force them to obey my every command. Impossible to control so many. Not forever."

I nodded.

"Learning to use and control your magic is going to take time," he said.

"Time we don't have."

"But we can teach you to suppress your magical signature so that they *think* you have control."

Hope flared. "I like the sound of that."

"Every supernatural learns to do it. Normally, it's easier. Less power equals less of a signature to control. But you have a lot of power."

"It's like trying not to stink when you sweat, isn't it?"

He chuckled. "Essentially."

"I can't even imagine how to do that."

"I'll help you. We started out the wrong way at La Papillon. I was trying to train you to use your magic—to compel it to do your will. But we need to start with something more attainable."

"And this is it."

"This is it."

"Why are they so interested in me?" I asked. "It seems overly aggressive."

"It is. They're normally intense about this kind of thing. But with you...there's something more to it." His gaze dropped to the crystal around my neck. It was tucked under my shirt, but I could feel its weight. "It likely has something to do with your ability to hold that."

"They want Orion's Heart?"

"Or they want you. You're strong enough to hold it, not anyone else."

Part of me wished I'd never grabbed this thing, but it had saved a woman's life. It had also marked me as a weirdo. Just like my actions at Police College. I'd used my powers too much then and made everyone suspicious.

Same here.

I pushed the chair back and stood. "Okay, let's get started. I'm going to learn to lock down this signature. I want to appear as powerful as a mouse."

He grinned. "That's the spirit."

I smiled back, liking this moment of camaraderie. We'd had a strange acquaintanceship so far, full of mistrust and attraction and life-saving deeds. Yet no dates or talking or normal stuff.

And I was still falling for him. Not in a normal way, as a product of normal experiences. No—in a strange way, one built of huge moments with mistrust in between.

I shook the thought away and looked at him. "What do I need to do?"

He stood and went to the window, then gestured for me to approach. "Come here."

I joined him, stopping a few inches away.

"Press your hand to my chest," he said. "I'm going to release my magical signature, and you'll feel it. When I draw it back into myself, try to focus on what that feels like. Use it as a guide for yourself."

More touching? I wasn't sure I could handle it.

I wasn't going to jump him or anything, but it certainly wasn't going to help me keep my distance from him.

He looked at me expectantly. There was no way I could say that in front of him, and so I raised my hand and pressed it to his chest, feeling the firmness of his muscles.

He drew in a quiet, unsteady breath.

His magic flared fiercely, and my knees nearly buckled. The firelight and whiskey scent of it swept through the room, followed by the sound of thunder. It was so loud it nearly deafened me, and I stumbled back.

"I'm sorry." He winced.

"I don't mind thunder."

"Thunder?" He looked outside.

The night was clear and bright.

"Your magic. It sounds like thunder."

"No. It sounds like the screams of the dying."

My eyes widened. "The screams of the what now?"

"The dying. And it feels like the icy grip of death."

"No, it feels like a warm…caress." I could feel it even now, stroking over me. This was one signature of his that I hadn't felt yet, and I wanted to lean into it. "And it smells like fire and whiskey."

"That's impossible. I know what my signature is. *Everyone* knows what it is."

I shrugged. "I know what I smell and hear, and it's not what you're describing. But if everyone thinks you feel like death, then I can see why you aren't the most popular guy in town."

A surprised laugh huffed out of him, and he met my gaze. "My magic really feels like that? Sounds like that?"

I nodded. "I like it."

"Strange. Signatures shouldn't be perceived differently by different people. They are what they are."

We were different. Our bond was different.

But I didn't say it.

I could see that he knew it—the way the knowledge flickered in his eyes and his jaw clenched.

Neither of us knew what to do with the bits of information we had. It didn't matter. The Cursed Mates thing had to wait. We had bigger problems, and I needed to practice controlling my signature. I also needed a long, hard nap if I wanted to survive and save Guild City.

"Let's get back to work," I said.

He nodded.

I pressed my hand firmly against his chest and focused on his magic. Again, he released it, and this time, I was ready. I still swayed slightly but didn't jump.

"I'm going to retract it now," he said.

I could feel it flow back into his body like water. His heart rate slowed slightly, and I focused on the feeling of his magic, trying to imagine doing the same with my own. When he'd pulled it all inside of himself, I could almost feel him building a wall within his soul.

"Wow." I whistled out a low breath. "Amazing. I can feel it."

"You try."

I mimicked what he'd done, trying to recreate it for myself. It went better than when I'd practiced with Eve and Mac. But then, they'd had a totally different method.

I liked Grey's better.

It took a few tries, but I improved.

"That's better," he said. "Now, keep that wall built inside you to contain it."

"I'll work on it." A yawn stole over me, and I reached up to stifle it.

"We need to rest."

I nodded. I was so tired, I could barely stand. "I'll get out of here."

"No." He gripped my arm, then released it quickly, looking startled. "The sorcerers will be out for blood."

I winced. "We need to explain to them what we were doing there."

"Miranda is trying. And if she doesn't succeed, I will. But right now, it's better if you're not wandering the streets alone after breaking into their tower. You don't want them to catch you."

"I really don't."

"There's another bedroom here. In the morning, we'll go together."

I nodded, wondering how I'd handle sleeping so close to Grey. *Could* I even sleep, as worked up as I was?

14

Grey

The next morning, I woke from dreams of Carrow. The sun was just rising, and the golden light reminded me of her hair.

Weak.

Disgusted, I dragged a hand over my head and climbed out of bed. So much had happened last night. My mind was still spinning, but I forced it to the back of my thoughts.

No time for that now.

I pulled on loose cotton pants and strode to the room where Carrow slept, passing the bookshelves that hadn't held my interest in years.

As I passed, one title caught my eye.

Poetry.

The faintest bit of interest flared, and I frowned.

That was odd.

I shook it away and went to her room, knocking on the door. "It's morning."

"I'll be out soon." Her voice sounded sleepy, and the idea of her curled up in bed made heat flash through me.

I returned to my room and had a record-quick shower, then dressed in dark trousers and a T-shirt, topping it with a black jacket. It'd be better to blend with the shadows, considering what was coming.

I tapped my comms charm. "Miranda?"

There was no response.

I frowned, hoping that she was safe. The sorcerers were highly unlikely to hurt her, and she could take care of herself. All the same, I worried.

A few moments later, I met Carrow in the living room. Her hair was damp from her shower. Miranda has brought her some clothes before heading to the Sorcerers' Guild—black jeans, T-shirt, and leather jacket, her usual uniform. We were dressed alike, I realized.

"You need to stop getting me clothes," she said.

"I don't see why."

"We're wearing the same outfit."

I cracked a smile. "Good. We'll blend in."

"You need to get back to your suits. We look like a weird match-matchy couple. This isn't Disney World."

We're not a couple. Never could be. "That's not really my scene."

"I can only imagine." She turned to the door. "Let's get out of here. Mac said they would meet us at eight. They found something."

We left my place and headed through town. It was early enough that the streets were quiet, but I kept my guard up anyway. The sorcerers tended to be night owls, but if Miranda hadn't convinced them to relax, I needed to be alert.

We reached Carrow's place a few minutes later, and she led me up the stairs to her small flat. It was nearly empty. A single couch was pushed against the wall, and the books that I'd brought her sat on one cushion.

Carrow looked between the books and me. "Thanks again."

I nodded. "Nice place."

"Mac is helping me furnish it."

"I like it."

"A bit different than your place."

"Nice all the same." I shrugged. "I don't much care for my place, anyway."

"The piano did look a bit dusty."

"It's been a while since I've had the interest."

She turned to me with a considering gaze, but said only, "Coffee?"

I nodded.

She brewed a pot as we waited, and by the time Mac,

Eve, and Quinn showed up, she had mugs poured for everyone.

Mac stepped into the room and raised a bag. "I brought muffins."

"Always thinking with her stomach." Eve grabbed the bag. Her raven followed her silently. "We found something, though."

Quinn gave me a long look, and I smiled coldly at him. I knew what he was thinking: I wasn't good enough for Carrow. As much as I hated it, I agreed.

The women sat on the couch, while Quinn and I leaned against the walls on opposite sides of the room. Carrow passed around the coffee mugs and took a muffin, then looked at Mac. "I hope you found something good, because we didn't get much, and it's supposed to happen tonight."

Mac leaned forward. "We talked to half a dozen people, and I used my powers on all of them. Two saw the dead guy hand off a key to someone else."

"And one of them heard mention of a magical power source." Eve looked at Carrow. "The power sources are like batteries. Small objects imbued with great power that can be used for spells."

"Similar to the ones used to power the spell that hides Guild City?" I asked.

"Just like." Eve nodded. "But a different one."

Quinn nodded. "They couldn't find the hidden ones, of course."

Naturally. I'd concealed them well when we'd installed the spell to protect Guild City. "How are the key and the power source connected?"

"The key opens the container where the power source is stored. Once it's out and they say the magic words..." Mac made a wide gesture with her hands. "Boom."

Carrow sat up straight. "It's the power source for the spell. I didn't get it before, but now I do."

"You know the spell?" Mac asked.

"Yes." I detailed our meeting with Mariketta and how I'd taken her memory, just like Ivan's goons had. "Once they have the power source out of the container, the spell will make the magic inside go haywire. The power will explode outward, taking down Black Church and the protective spell that hides us."

"We need to beat them to it," Quinn said.

We had no idea where they were now, but... "They'll be at the church tonight," I told the others.

"We'll go wait for them," Eve said.

Carrow frowned. "Mariketta said we had to go under to approach."

"What does that mean?" Mac asked.

"I honestly don't know. And she said we could only make it through at dusk."

"That's too late," said Eve. "We need to get there earlier. Like, now."

"Agreed," I began, but before I could elaborate, a

massive shockwave rushed through the air, nearly sending me to my knees.

Mac yelped in surprise, and a ceramic cup hit the floor and shattered. Outside, people shouted and screamed in alarm.

Carrow sprang up from the couch, her eyes wild. "What was that?"

"I have no idea." I strode to the window. A massive, glowing blue dome rose over the rooftops of Guild City near the Black Church. The dome was partially transparent but sparked with magic. "It's started."

Carrow hurried up and peered out. "Holy crap. What is that?"

"A protective shield," said Mac, a scowl in her voice. "They've put it up so we can't get in."

"We need to evacuate the city," Carrow replied.

"They're trying," Quinn said. "But it takes time, especially with so many supernaturals who can't blend with society. And not everyone believes in the threat."

I pointed to the dome out the window. "*That* will make them believe."

"Fair point," he allowed. "But what about those who can't leave? The ones tied to this place by their magic?"

"We need to stop this before it happens," said Carrow, then sprinted for the door and down the stairs.

We followed, the four of us racing down the street after her. Supernaturals spilled out of their houses, staring in fright at the dome hovering over the center of town, trapping untold numbers inside.

Carrow led the way, weaving through the streets swiftly and accurately. We reached the edge of the dome moments later. It gleamed transparent blue, like glassy water, and arced over a huge section of town.

On the other side, people ran screaming out of their houses, horror on their faces.

"They're trapped." Carrow reached up and touched the dome with her fingertips. Sparks flared, and she yelped, drawing her hand back.

"There's no way through," I said. "Not as long as the magic works."

"Those people can't escape." Eve's voice trembled.

Carrow turned to me, eyes bright. "That's what Mariketta meant! We can reach the Church by going *under* the dome." She frowned. "But how? Do we dig?"

"The Dwarves' Guild," Mac said.

I nodded. "She's right. They own most of the tunnels under the city. They'll know how to get through."

"Where are they?" Carrow asked. "Do they have a tower we can go to?"

"Not a normal tower," said Eve. "But we can arrange a meeting."

"We'll go now," I said.

"You can get us in this early?" Mac shook her head. "Of *course* you can. What am I thinking?"

"I'm going to check on the shifters trying to evacuate," Quinn said. "I'll meet you later. Don't go without me."

"We'll call," Mac assured him.

He nodded and turned, striding down the street in the direction of his guild tower.

Carrow looked at me. "Lead the way."

Carrow

Grey strode ahead, guiding us down the winding streets toward a part of town that I'd never visited before. The streets became quieter, the buildings slightly larger.

"This is the posh side of the city," Mac said. "Old money over here."

There were no shops on the bottom floors of the buildings, just quiet doors and windows with pretty curtains and flowers in the window boxes. The stately houses were two or three stories tall and attractive. Many of the Tudor fronts had been replaced with newer exteriors of plaster and brick, though they were still at least three hundred years old, from the looks of them.

"They like it here because the Dwarves' Guild tower is so quiet," Mac said. "But they're snobs."

Everything *did* look quite stiff and perfect. Particularly the clearing that was common in front of every guild tower. This one was lovely, tended grass with pebble pathways and flower beds. Everything was symmetrical and precise.

"Too perfect for me," I murmured.

"Designed by some famous landscape architect centuries ago," Eve said. "Only residents of this neighborhood are allowed to use it."

"Are they Dwarves like Snow White's dwarves or Tolkien's dwarves?"

"There are some similarities there," Eve said. "They do prefer it underground, and mining *is* their primary source of wealth."

"Wealth being the operative word," Mac said. "They have a *lot* of it, and they know how to use it."

We stopped in front of the short, squat tower. It was only two stories tall and built of massive stones. The windows looked empty, and the entire place vibrated with an eerie quiet.

"Is it abandoned?" I asked.

"No. But most of the activity happens underground," Mac said.

Grey turned to us. "Ready?"

Mac leaned close and whispered in my ear, "Try to hide your signature. We don't want them knowing how powerful you are."

I concentrated, attempting to mimic what I'd done last night with Grey.

"That's good," Mac said. "You're getting a lot better."

I looked at Grey. "Ready."

The others nodded, and he knocked on the heavy wooden door. A moment later, it swung open, revealing a lovely room papered in silk and floored with gleaming wood. We entered, and I spotted a short, stout man hurrying through the entryway.

He stopped and stared at us. His long beard was carefully braided and threaded through with gold and gems. The maroon suit that he wore was perfectly tailored, and his neon green tie somehow complimented it despite the garish shade. He was the most dapper man I'd ever seen.

"Hello, Perowall." Grey's smile did not reach his eyes.

Perowall's brows rose. "Devil. It's been a while since you've dined with us. But I'm afraid we're not open."

Dined? Opened?

Mac must have spotted the confusion on my face. Leaning closer, she whispered, "They run the most famous restaurant in town. The Cellar."

"Could you please make a special request of Ogden the Bold?" Grey's voice was firm. "We'd very much appreciate it. We'll make it worth his while."

"I'll see what I can do." He disappeared behind a heavy velvet curtain.

"I've never eaten here," Mac said. "I hear it's really quite good."

"And it's doing double duty as a meeting place to beg for help in stopping the apocalypse," I said.

Mac shrugged. "That's Guild City for you."

"I doubt we'll be eating, Mac," Eve said. "So get your head out of your stomach."

"Fine, fine."

I met Grey's eyes, but they were unreadable.

A few moments later, Perowall returned. "If you'll please come with me, Ogden will see you."

Thank God.

We followed Perowall down a wide staircase to a lower level. The air cooled as we descended, and I got the impression of a huge underground space, even though we were only in the stairwell.

"No one knows how big their tower really is," Mac whispered. "It extends underground. Not to mention The Below."

"The Below?"

"The tunnels."

"Right."

Perowall led us into a long, narrow room with an arched brick ceiling. Small tables lined each side, covered in creamy linen with lovely flower arrangements. Golden light glowed throughout, giving it a distinctly romantic feel.

Perowall led us to a large table at the end, where he gestured for us to sit. He slipped away before we'd done so, but Ogden appeared a moment later. His beard was even longer and more intricately braided than Perowall's, studded with dozens of gleaming gems. It looked like the dwarven version of a crown, albeit upside down. His suit was as fabulous as Perowall's, a brilliant cobalt with a canary yellow tie.

"Devil." Ogden inclined his head in greeting and sat at the head of the long table. "To what do we owe this pleasure?"

To what do we owe this pleasure?

He was really playing it cool, considering the situation.

"We're here to request your aid." Grey gestured to the three of us. "I'm sure you know Mac and Eve. This is Carrow."

Ogden nodded at my friends, then pinned me with a gaze. "Never met you before."

"I'm new." His intense scrutiny made me uncomfortable. Could he sense my magic?

"Hmm." He turned his attention to Grey. "What kind of help? Does this have anything to do with those miserable sorcerers and that magical dome outside?"

"They've been here?" Grey sounded surprised.

"Indeed, they have." He grumbled. "Bastards."

I leaned toward Mac and whispered, "What's the deal there?"

"Longstanding grudge. Hundreds of years old."

"What did they want?" Grey asked.

"The same thing that you want, I presume." Ogden gave a knowing smile. "They wanted help navigating the tunnels to Black Church. But we'd never help those bastards."

So the sorcerers *were* trying to help. Mariketta must have convinced them of the threat. Except these Dwarves were damned stubborn in their dislike of the sorcerers.

"It's a matter of life and death," I said.

"For you, perhaps," Ogden said.

"Don't you care that the city could be destroyed?" I demanded, unable to keep my mouth shut. "Your home?"

"This is my home." He gestured to the restaurant around us. "And the rest of The Below. The explosion can't reach underground."

I tried to keep the horror off my face. "You'd live under a city of corpses and rubble."

He shrugged. "That is not ideal, but we've got all our manpower busy shoring up the surface portions of our domain. We don't have time to help you."

"We can stop this," I said. "If you can get us there, you won't have to worry about bodies or destruction."

Grey leaned forward. "I know you're not particularly fond of the surface and that you'd survive down here even if it disappeared, but life would be better for you if that never happened. You can't deny it. Just spare us one person to lead us to Black Church. That's all."

Ogden scowled and muttered to himself, then said, "You'll have to pay."

"I'll take care of it," Grey said.

The Dwarf looked at the four of us. "All of you."

I frowned. "What do you want?"

"Money from him." Ogden nodded to Grey. "Potions from Eve, a vision from Mac. And what can you do?"

"I can read information from objects and people."

"A psychic, eh?"

"Yes." It wasn't an exact description, but let him believe it. "I'll read any object you like."

He pursed his lips. "Good. Payment first."

"No." Grey's voice was firm. "You'll have the money first—I'll see to the transfer—but we need to begin immediately. Time is of the essence."

Ogden grumbled, then nodded. "Make the transfer."

Grey stood and strode toward the stairs, raising the comms charm at his wrist to his lips. His voice drifted away as he spoke.

Mac pulled out her mobile and began to surreptitiously type a text message. I caught sight of Quinn's name. She was telling him that it was time.

Ogden's eyes moved to me. "You've got quite a bit of magic there, girl."

Girl?

Normally, I'd bite a man's head off that, but this wasn't a normal situation. We needed his help. I gave him a pinched smile and doubled down on my signature.

Fortunately, Grey returned a moment later with

another Dwarf attired in an emerald-green suit with a magenta tie. I was starting to sense a trend.

"It is done," Grey said.

The shorter man next to him nodded. "The money has gone through."

"Thank you, Fortirue." Ogden nodded. "Devil."

"Shall we leave?" Grey asked.

"It seems it is time." Ogden clapped his hands and hopped up. Grabbing a last bite of cheese from the plate, he popped it in his mouth.

"Excellent," Grey said. "My men will be here in one moment."

Ogden frowned. "Your men?"

"We're attempting to break into Black Church to stop a black magic bomb," he replied with a raised brow. "Wouldn't you bring backup?"

15

CARROW

A black magic *bomb.*

Grey's words echoed in my mind.

This was the real deal. Just a week ago, my life had been normal. Now I was here, running toward a black magic bomb.

We returned to the main tower where we'd entered the Dwarves' Guild. Grey's security forces arrived a moment later, a dozen shifters wearing identical black special-ops wear. There were roughly equal numbers of men and women, strong and capable looking, with firm jaws and serious eyes. The shifters were perfect for this work.

Quinn arrived last, nodding at the other shifters

before joining us. His dark hair was tousled, as if he'd run all the way.

"Are we ready?" Ogden grumbled.

Grey nodded. "Ready."

Ogden turned and led us through another door. Grey and I followed closely, my friends behind us. His shifter guards took the rear, and we made our way deep underground, following the wide staircase to an even wider tunnel.

"This is The Below," Ogden said. "Territory of the Dwarves, and don't you forget it."

"Thank you for permitting us entrance," Grey said.

Ogden muttered and started down the stone-lined tunnel. As he walked, his clothing transformed from a dapper suit to rugged clothing suited to a miner—albeit in the same bright blue and yellow. It should have looked silly, but somehow, Ogden pulled it off.

The underground space was lit by golden lamps that shone on the stone walls and ground. A fine carpet ran down the middle of the hall, and the doors on either side were made of beautifully carved wood. All were shut, but magic seemed to spill out of the cracks, different scents and sounds that lit up my imagination.

What was happening behind those doors? This whole place made me want to explore, but we kept up a fast pace that made it impossible.

One door was open, however, revealing an enormous cavern and a glowing blue waterfall. Gems seemed to glitter from the stone in every shade of the rainbow, and the pool of water looked inviting.

"Wow." I leaned toward Mac and whispered. "Have you ever been here?"

"No. It's hard to get past the restaurant."

We passed another open room. I peered in, spotting a gorgeous library full of thousands of books. The shelves soared toward the ceiling, dotted with tall ladders here and there. Plush armchairs sat in front of a roaring fire, and magic seemed to sparkle in the air. It was utterly fantastic, and I itched to get inside.

"That looks amazing." Eve's eyes gleamed with interest, and I remembered her book collection from earlier.

For the first time ever, I didn't see her raven at her side. Now that I thought of it, the bird had disappeared once we'd entered the Dwarves' Guild. "Your raven isn't here."

She shot me an annoyed look. "I've told you and everyone else a million times, I don't know what you're talking about."

Her tone was so exasperated that I believed her, though *how* she could miss the raven was beyond me. Did it appear to everyone but her?

Eventually, the lovely hall gave way to more rustic tunnels. The lights were spaced farther apart, and the carpet and doorways disappeared. From the sides, earthen tunnels diverged off the main passage, stretching far into the distance. It was too dark to see what they led to, but my imagination ran wild.

Mac leaned close. "There are rumors of gems down here. Gold, too."

"In *London*?"

"Crazy, right?"

I nodded.

"It's said they've always been here," Eve whispered. "But the Dwarves kept them hidden from humans with magic. Now they mine it for themselves."

Eventually, the main tunnel joined with a more modern one. A track ran down the middle of the cement floor, and the arched ceiling was inset with electric lights that flickered weakly.

"Is this part of the Underground?" I asked.

Ogden looked back. "It's human. Some of these are abandoned from World War II. Destroyed in the Blitz. Others are still used but exist on a slightly different plane. They're shadows."

"Shadows?"

A rumbling noise cut off the thought, and Ogden darted to the wall and pressed himself against it.

"Come on." Grey did the same, and the rest of us followed.

Bright lights blared from up ahead, speeding toward us.

"Holy crap, a train?" I squeezed myself hard against the wall.

"Not quite," Ogden said. "Getting hit wouldn't kill you, but it doesn't feel nice."

The train zoomed by, loud enough to make my head hurt. A rush of wind whipped my hair around, and the side of the train car passed two feet from my nose. It was oddly transparent, like a ghost.

Beside me, Mac slowly reached out a hand, letting the train rush through her fingertips. Heart pounding, I did the same. It stung but didn't leave a mark.

Finally, the train passed.

I sagged against the wall, heart still pounding.

"That was wild," Eve said.

"We need to keep moving." Ogden pushed himself off the wall.

He led us through endless tunnels, several of which had been damaged by bomb blasts. Tumbled rubble and bricks were a haunting reminder of man's inhumanity. But then again, supernaturals weren't any better. This Ivan fellow was going to blow up an entire city, simply as part of a vendetta against Grey.

After two hours of walking, I said, "This seems to be much bigger than Guild City itself."

"It is," Ogden replied. "The tunnels take a circuitous route, so we're covering far more ground."

We passed a dark tunnel to the right, and movement sounded from inside. A rough scraping, like stone against stone. Or shifting rubble.

Ogden shouted into the darkness. "That you, Jack?"

A shrieking laugh from within made the hair on my arms stand on end. I shivered, squinting into the dark.

The Dwarf reached into one of his many pockets and withdrew a lighter and a little metal canister. They didn't look like magical charms to me.

The laughter sounded again, and Ogden said, "I'd step back if I were you. Jack has sharp claws."

I retreated onto the tracks, keeping an ear out for the sound of an oncoming train. The odd laughter came closer and closer.

I leaned toward Mac. "Do you know who Jack is?"

"No idea."

"It's Spring-heeled Jack," Grey said. "A bogeyman from Victorian times. He used to terrorize the humans in London until the witches trapped him down here."

"That old urban legend?" I asked, vaguely remembering.

"A legend, yes. But a true one," Grey said. "Same for the pigs."

My eyebrows rose as I looked at him. "The pigs?"

"Another urban legend that's true. Slightly later than the Victorian period. It says there's a herd of feral pigs down here."

"That's hogwash," Ogden said. "No pun intended."

"You just don't want anyone coming down and hunting them," Mac said.

Ogden grumbled, and I could almost sense the truth to the rumbling noise. Another laugh sounded, shrill and close. From the shadows, a slender, cloaked figure leapt out. A manic grin stretched across the skinny face, and the eyes gleamed like fire. Long claws tipped the ends of its fingers, and the creature leapt two meters into the air as it approached.

I flinched backward as Ogden flicked on his lighter and pressed the button on the metal canister. An enormous jet of flame shot out, and Jack shrieked and scuttled back into the dark.

"You just have to speak his language," Ogden said.

My heartbeat thundered as I searched the darkness for Jack. I could hear him scuttling about, laughing and muttering to himself. He really was the stuff of nightmares.

"Come on, now." Ogden turned and strode past Jack's tunnel, continuing down the old Underground line toward our destination. He shouted to the back of our queue, "Hurry up at the rear! Jack recovers quickly. You don't want to meet those claws."

I heard a few of the shifters growl. I had a feeling they'd be a good match for Jack. As we continued down the tunnel, we passed Tube stations that I recognized. The platforms were empty, though they shouldn't be at this hour.

"Why are the platforms empty?" I asked.

"These are shadow stations," Ogden said. "Just like the train. There are people at the real station, most likely—but we're not really there. Our territory was expanded into the human realm using our magic."

I met Grey's eyes and whispered, "So there were magical Dwarves in the Tube lines when I was riding from place to place?"

"In a sense," Grey said. "It's like how the Fae realms are located on earth but in a different realm. Two realities on the same piece of land—human and Fae—neither ever seeing the other."

Scarcely able to wrap my mind around that, I turned to Eve. "Can I visit one?"

"Maybe." She smiled a bit sadly. "Not mine, though. Even I'm not allowed back there."

I shot her a sympathetic look and stored the info away for later, glancing back at the Tube station that we'd nearly left. It was nicely familiar.

Unfamiliar, however, was the horrible scent that filled the tunnels.

"Dark magic," Grey said. "Coming from Black Church, no doubt."

I covered my nose with my shirt, breathing shallowly. It got worse as we walked, becoming a horrible prickling sensation against my skin.

We passed places where the Tube lines seemed to connect. The District line crossed with the Central line, which should be impossible. Not only would the trains crash, but those two lines never even met at a station.

"How are they crossing?" I asked.

"Magic. Part of our empire," Ogden said. "They wouldn't be much use to us if we could access them all easily. No need to transfer at stations. We can stick to the tunnels and make our way all over London."

Holy crap. My head spun with the idea that there were dapper Dwarves under every bit of London.

Soon, the tunnel ahead of us began to glow with a faint blue light. As we neared, I spotted the same barrier I'd seen arching up over the town.

"Those bastards," Ogden muttered, stopping in front of it.

"It looks like they can affect The Below as well," Mac said. "Aren't you glad you helped us?"

Ogden grumbled. "I don't like the look of this."

Carefully, I reached out to touch the barrier. It pricked sharply against my fingers, burning. "It's not as bad as it was on the surface, but we can't walk through."

"I'll be leaving you here." Ogden backed away. "I've things to see to."

"I paid you to take us all the way," Grey said.

"I'll reimburse you." Ogden shook his head. "No way I'm tangling with whatever is down there. This is dark, and I have things that need doing."

"Hiding away all his treasure," Mac murmured.

He did have shifty eyes, but I had seen the same kind of panic on fellow recruits at police training. He was spooked, and there was no coming back from it.

"Tell us how to reach Black Church, at least," I begged.

"You're nearly there, but it's complicated," he said. "Try to follow the dark magic."

That was too difficult. Too uncertain. "What human Tube station is it near? I can find that."

Ogden frowned. "It's closest to Hyde Park Corner on our magical grid, though you'd never find it if you were above ground."

"Which way?"

"Southbound from that station."

I nodded. "Thanks. We'll take it from here."

His gaze moved to the magical barrier behind us. "If you can get through that."

I faced the barrier, my skin itching from my proximity. It really was repellent.

Ogden left, his footsteps echoing into the distance as the five of us stood in a line, staring at the magical shield. The twelve shifters of Declan's security team waited silently behind us, all at attention.

"I could try to blast it with my lightning," Eve offered.

"It's dusk now, according to the time," I said. "Mariketta said we could cross at dusk."

"Might as well try," Quinn said.

No one else had any ideas, so we stepped back and watched as Eve raised her hand. Her hair seemed to prickle with white light, which arced down her arm.

Thunder cracked as it burst from her hand, shooting into the barrier.

The shining white bolt collided with the shield, and the force of it blasted us all backward. I landed hard, pain screaming through me, then scrambled upright, my head ringing.

The barrier stood strong and undamaged.

Grey rose gracefully, striding toward it. He picked up speed, his footsteps pounding the ground. His speed blew my mind, and when he plowed into the barrier, he broke through with sheer force.

It sent another shock wave toward us, slightly weaker this time. I stumbled backward, watching him appear on the other side.

He turned to us, face tight. "I don't recommend that. Hurts like hell."

I approached, staring at him through the barrier. It made his form appear wavy, as if I were looking through water.

"Step aside." A gravelly voice sounded from behind me.

I turned to see the biggest of his shifter guards preparing to run through the barrier. Quinn shot him a look like he was crazy, then got out of his way. I did the same, clearing the path.

The shifter charged, transforming into a bear as he ran. His gleaming brown fur rippled over enormous muscles as he hurtled toward the barrier. He moved like a steam train, and I watched in awe as he slammed into the barrier.

And bounced off.

I stumbled back, forced by the reverberation of the shockwave.

The bear groaned, then rolled over and stood on shaky legs.

"I'm out," Mac said. "If the bear can't do it, none of us can."

I looked toward Grey. He was the strongest by far, but he couldn't face down Ivan's whole team alone.

From the look in his eyes, though, that was exactly what he planned to do. Frustrated, I approached the barrier again.

"Carrow, don't." He held out his hand. "It's too difficult."

"I'm not going to try to blast my way through like you did." I knew my limitations.

And my strengths.

I just needed to understand the barrier better.

I raised my hand, hovering it over the shimmering surface, not quite touching.

How do I get through you?

Would my magic work without touch? Could I possibly figure this out?

A vision flashed in my mind, bright and pure: a light, gleaming from a tiny crystal.

Orion's Heart, hanging on the chain around my

neck, suddenly felt heavy and solid. I reached for it, pulled it up, and slipped it over my head. The chain dangled from my hand as I raised the crystal to the barrier.

"Careful," Grey said.

The barrier pricked painfully against my hand as I pressed the crystal into it. It was definitely weaker down here, as Mariketta had said. It felt even weaker than it had been when I'd touched it just moments ago. Dusk must be fully here.

Orion's Heart seemed to warm, softening the barrier, almost melting it. I pushed hard, forcing my entire arm through the now gelatinous barrier. I kept pushing, and soon, I stood on the other side.

Grey's eyes moved between the crystal and me, and I shrugged.

"Hey, help a girl out," Mac's voice sounded from the other side of the barrier, and I turned.

She grinned at me and stretched out a hand.

I wrapped my fingers around the crystal and reached for her. "Grab my wrist, not the crystal."

If I was the only one who could hold it, I didn't want it to hurt her. The barrier prickled against my hand as I forced it though. On the other side, Mac gripped my wrist. I pulled her through, having to put some serious muscle into it.

She popped out on our side.

"Nice work." She grinned widely and released my wrist.

I repeated the movement fourteen more times, pulling through Quinn and Eve and each of the shifters. Finally, we all stood on the proper side.

The shifters eyed me warily, and I turned away, uncomfortable. They looked at me like I'd done something impossible.

"You'll speak of this to no one." Grey's voice brooked no argument.

There was a murmurer of assent as I turned and stared down the tunnel. "We need to get to the Hyde Park Corner Station. Follow me."

Grey joined me as I led the group farther down the tunnels.

"I don't know where the Dwarves have magically joined the lines, so we'll try to go the normal route." I searched my memory of the lines and stations, then groaned. "It'll take hours, though. We're pretty far away."

"We don't have hours."

We came to a magical intersection. The lines crossed here, no station needed, and I swore I could see the Dwarves' magic working at the seams where each tunnel joined the other.

I racked my memory. "If we go north, it should cut off a lot of time. Maybe."

"How sure are you?" Grey asked.

"The alternative is a two-hour jog that will make us too late. So I'm sure enough." Confidence surged through me. I turned to head south.

The group followed, and we hurried along. It took two more turns down two different lines, but I felt the dark magic grow stronger. We were on the right track. "We're nearly there. Hyde Park Corner is up ahead."

Sure enough, we passed through the ghostly station and kept heading north. Within a hundred meters, we reached a darker section of the tunnels. Black slime coated the walls, and the magic reeked so badly that my stomach pitched.

I stared into the darkness, a shiver racing over my skin. "We're here."

16

Grey

She'd done it. Carrow had directed us through the ghostly Tube lines, flawlessly locating the base of Black Church.

I searched the area ahead of us, grimacing at the stench. The black slime covering the walls of the station was unusual.

"Where's the entrance?" Carrow asked.

Mac hurried ahead, shining a lightstone ring on the walls of the tunnel, and avoiding the largest puddles of slime. "I see nothing here."

The shifters spread out, searching for a secret door.

"Hang on." Carrow pointed to a small animal

running down the tracks toward us. "Something is coming."

"That's the biggest sewer rat I've ever seen," Quinn said.

The animal neared, then stopped and stood upright. It hissed at Quinn. *Who are you calling a rat?*

"That's Cordelia, Quinn," Carrow said. "My familiar. She doesn't like being called a rat."

"My apologies, Cordelia." Quinn frowned. "I didn't recognize you from a distance."

Hmm. I'm not impressed.

I glanced at Quinn, who still frowned. "Can't you hear her?" I asked.

"No." Quinn looked at me like I was crazy. "She's Carrow's familiar, not mine."

Carrow shot me a surprised look. "Can *you* hear her?"

Dare I tell her? I hadn't been able to hear Cordelia earlier, but now I could.

I didn't answer, and Carrow's expression suggested she wanted to talk about this later. She turned to Cordelia. "Do you know how to get in?"

Of course. I know all the good ways into all the best places.

Again, I understood her. What the hell was going on? Only a familiar's person could understand them.

Cordelia shot me a keen glance, her black eyes gleaming. *What are you looking at, Fang Boy?*

Fang Boy?

I felt my eyebrows rise halfway up my head. Unexpectedly, a laugh almost burst from me.

A raccoon had just called me Fang Boy. It'd been centuries since anyone had so much as considered disrespecting me. Even the sorcerers treaded lightly, though they often hurled spells while they did so.

But this raccoon feared no vampire.

The absurdity of it made the corner of my mouth crack up in a smile.

Carrow stared at me, eyes wide. She mouthed, "Fang Boy?"

Come on. No time to dally. Those egg-sucking rat bastards are hard at work up there.

"Let's get a move on," Carrow said.

Cordelia nodded, then turned on her back feet and ran about ten meters down the way. She made a sharp right and dove into what appeared to be a pit. *You have to go down to go up*, she explained, her voice echoing out.

I went first, climbing down a ladder into a narrow tunnel that extended five meters to the side. At the end, a long tunnel led upward. Another ladder was bolted to the wall, and Cordelia was already halfway up.

Carrow appeared behind me, and I could just barely catch the lavender smell of her magic. She was so much better at controlling her signature. Safer for her, but I missed the scent.

"Be careful," I said.

"You too." She grinned. "Fang Boy."

"Let's not make it a thing."

"Sure." She winked. "Now get climbing."

I turned and hurried up the ladder, following the fat raccoon to the top. A trap door blocked us, and Cordelia disappeared, climbing right through the wood like a ghost.

I pushed on the wooden door and emerged into a dank, dark room that had to be in the dungeons. I pulled my lightstone out of my pocket and raised it high.

"We're in a cell." Carrow's voice sounded from below. She'd popped her head up though the trapdoor and quickly climbed out.

I strode to the iron door and pushed on it. With a shrieking creak, it swung open.

"Who's there?" a rough voice sounded.

Shite.

I shoved my lightstone back into my pocket and let my night vision take over. I'd lost my ability to see color when I'd been turned, but I could see in the dark, which compensated for it. Fortunately, I hadn't lost my night vision when I'd regained the full spectrum of color.

Behind me, the team was almost silent as they crept from the tunnel down below. I strode quickly down the hall, searching for the voice.

Near the front of the dungeon by the stairs where they'd kept Carrow, four members of the Council were locked in a cell.

My brows rose.

"*You*," Ubhan hissed. "You've done this."

"Hardly," I said. "We're here to help."

"You're being an idiot, Ubhan," Mateo said. "He wasn't there when they came."

"We're here to stop them. How many are there?" I asked.

"Get us out of here," Ubhan demanded.

"I'm looking for a key," Mac's voice sounded from nearby.

"Me, too," Carrow said.

"It's at the end of the hall, in the alcove!" Ubhan shouted.

I turned to Carrow. "There should be a pair of powerful Magicuffs there. They're reinforced with Elvish steel."

Mateo's gaze met mine. "You want the Elvish cuffs?"

"For their leader. He's immortal. Impossible to kill, even with trauma."

"They should be hidden," Mateo said to Carrow. "A stone box in the back right corner."

"I'll find them." She disappeared.

I turned back to Mateo. "Tell me what you know about them."

"There were over two dozen men that we saw," Mateo said. "Scattered throughout the church, setting up a spell of some kind. The leaders said something about the alcoves off the main room."

"I got the cuffs, but we couldn't find a key," Carrow said.

"And we need to get a move on," Mac said. "I feel the dark magic growing."

She was right. It pulsed like an oily sickness, polluting every breath.

"There's a key in my office, on the second floor," Ubhan said.

I looked at my guards and pointed to James, a wolf shifter. "Go find it. Let them out."

Ubhan scowled. "You're sending just one?"

"We need every person we have to fight Ivan."

"You know he's right," Mateo said.

"Kiss arse," Ubhan hissed.

I left them to it, striding toward the stairs. Carrow joined me, along with her friends and my crew, and handed me the cuffs. At the main level, I hesitated, listening for anything out of the ordinary.

Sound came from main church.

Chanting.

"He's started the spell," said Carrow, and sprinted forward.

We raced after her, moving silently through the entrance hall of the church. The doors to the main hall were open, and we could see right into the round space.

Ivan stood in the center, surrounded by a dozen guards. There were six alcoves situated around the edges of the main room, alcoves that were normally empty. From our vantage point, I could only see three. But each contained three of Ivan's men, hurriedly marking something on the floor with glowing paint.

I turned to my guards. "You lot take out the men in the alcoves. We'll deal with Ivan."

He and his personal guards stood in the middle, atop the bronze star. The floor around him had been painted with an enormous symbol. Its intricate lines were impossible to see well from here, but it would have taken hours to paint it.

Though I hadn't encountered Ivan in years, he looked as I remembered him: tall and wiry, with white hair and a manic glow to his eyes. It was even worse now, as if centuries underwater had polluted his mind even more.

They probably had.

He held a key in one hand and an intricate metal box in the other. As he chanted, he moved the key toward the box.

Carrow and I sprinted for him. Fear for her made my blood chill and my heart race. At my side, the shifter Quinn transformed into a panther. He ran alongside Carrow, sprinting ahead of her to block her from anything Ivan's guards might throw her way.

I didn't like Quinn, but I appreciated his loyalty. Anyone who protected Carrow was fine by me. Still, I felt the oddest pang of jealousy.

Mac drew her sword from the ether and charged.

Eve's wings unfurled behind her, glittering and bright. She launched herself into the air, raising a hand that crackled with lighting. Thunder boomed as she hurled a bolt at one of the guards who'd started to attack. It slammed into him, sending him to the ground.

Ivan raised a hand, making a broad gesture that formed a small magical dome around him. It gleamed transparent blue, like the protective barrier that had kept us out of Black Church.

Mac clashed with one of the guards, her sword swinging. She took off his head with one powerful blow, then whirled to find another target. Quinn took out another, leaping for his throat.

From the left, another guard hurled a fireball the size of a small car. It plowed toward me. I powered through, calling upon protective magic I used rarely and only when attacked by fire.

The flames slammed into me, sending pain singing through my veins. I absorbed the heat, transferring it into energy so that I could run faster. I couldn't take hits like this indefinitely—it weakened me eventually—but in battle, it was a handy talent. Maybe it was the ice in my veins, but fire wasn't as harmful to me as it was to others.

Around me, the sounds of battle rose. Out of the corner of my vision, I saw my guards transform into animals—lions, bears, wolves. They attacked Ivan's men, scattering them throughout the church.

Ivan stood under his protective dome, still chanting. He was turning the key in the lock now. My heartbeat thundered.

We were too late.

Ivan had prepared the spell. All that remained now was for him to finish it.

Carrow

I sprinted alongside Grey, racing for Ivan. Mariketta's spell had been long and complicated, and he was already nearing the end.

Beneath my feet, the paint glowed with magic. It grew brighter as Ivan chanted, energy flowing out from the container that he was unlocking. I could feel it vibrating as the lid slowly opened, revealing a brilliant glow from within.

On my chest, Orion's Heart began to pulse in tandem, like it was responding to the magic.

Overhead, Eve swooped through the air, avoiding blasts shot by a fire mage while trying to take him out with her lightning. Quinn made quick work of another guard, taking him down and tearing out his throat. Mac moved like a ghost, quick and precise with her blade.

More men seemed to be appearing from the alcoves, more backup than I'd expected.

Grey neared the barrier that protected Ivan, moving like a train as he crashed through the transparent blue wall. I followed. Gripping the gem in my hand, I smashed through after him.

Pain blazed through me as I forced my way to the other side. I skidded to a stop in front of Ivan.

The man's wild eyes met mine, and he laughed. In front of him, the power source shone and pulsed with magic. It was the size of my fist and had risen out of its container entirely. The key lay discarded on the ground, and the intricate box dropped to the floor with a clatter, leaving the glowing orb hovering a foot above Ivan's head.

Overhead, the star-shaped window in the ceiling opened. The blinding light from the power source shot into the sky, spearing through the opening.

"It is done." Ivan laughed. His eyes were glued to Grey. "There is no stopping the spell, *Devil.*" He threw out his hand, sending a blast of magic at us.

I ducked, taking the blast partially to the shoulder. It threw me backward, slamming me into the ground. I skidded painfully across the stone.

Aching, I scrambled upright. The blast had thrown Grey off his balance. Ivan made a run for it, but the vampire was too fast. He lunged toward Ivan and grabbed him by the throat.

I sprinted for the glowing power source. It pulsed with magic, going wild as the power inside started to spin out of control.

"You're not going anywhere," Grey growled. He grappled with Ivan, trying to get something out of his hand.

A transport charm.

The bastard was going to try to transport out of here, leaving us all to blow up. He'd have to make it out of the church to use the charm, though.

I left Grey to it. The fighting men were only two meters from me, but my attention was on the pulsing power source.

How the hell did I stop it?

Shaking, I reached out to touch it.

"No!" Mac screamed. "It's too powerful."

But I didn't have a choice.

I had the spell in my mind. And Mariketta had said that I had everything I needed.

What did she mean? I had nothing except my ability to read objects.

I'd have to risk it.

As my fingertip neared the gem, it burned with heat. All around, the battle raged. I had eyes only for the glowing stone that threatened to take us all out. With every second that passed, it vibrated more fiercely, sending out waves of magic that made my stomach pitch.

My fingertip collided with the gem, and I forced my

magic to do my bidding, calling it up from the deepest recesses of my mind.

An image flashed—me, chanting the spell in reverse.

Reverse?

Why the hell hadn't I thought of that?

It could undo what Ivan had started—at least partially. The power source was primed to blow, *now*. But if I could undo enough of the spell to get the stone back into the box, it would be contained. Controlled.

We'd be safe.

I just had to get that damned box.

The intricately carved box and key lay scattered on the stone where Ivan had dropped them. He and Grey were locked in a battle of magical assaults punctuated by flying fists. In their scuffle, Ivan nearly stepped on the box.

"No!" Fear pulsed. We needed that. I lunged for it, taking a kick to the head that made me see stars.

I curled myself around the box and tried to roll out of the way.

Grey roared and yanked at Ivan, dragging him away ferociously. The power with which he fought shocked me.

I grabbed the key and got to my feet.

I squeezed my eyes shut to better remember the spell, trying to drag it up from the depths of my memory. It was so long and complicated—and I had to recite it backward?

In my mind, I sent myself back to Mariketta's strange room. I recalled touching her temple and absorbing the spell. It came to my lips, spilling forth. As the sounds of battle raged, I chanted the spell in reverse.

The dark magic that pulsed in the air began to lessen. The beam of light that shot through the window in the ceiling retracted.

"No!" Ivan shouted.

I spoke faster, the words tumbling over themselves. I held out the open box, praying this would work. As I neared the end of the spell, I opened my eyes.

The glowing orb was dimmer now, not as blinding. It floated down toward the box that I held. My heart thundered in anticipation.

In the distance, Ivan struggled to break free of Grey's headlock. The battle was fierce since both men were immortal—Ivan even more so, since trauma apparently could not kill him.

The power source fitted itself neatly into the box, and I snapped the lid shut. Quickly, I cranked the key in the lock.

The dark magic stopped pulsing.

The window in the ceiling closed.

The spell was dead.

Ivan roared in rage. Magic vibrated through the sound, shaking the room so violently that I fell to my knees. Power exploded out of Ivan. It threw Grey across the room, slamming him into the side wall with enough force to crack the stones.

"Grey!" I yelled.

Ivan charged at me, fury on his face.

I scrambled upright and screamed, "Eve!"

My friend appeared above, flying just below the ceiling. I chucked the key and box upward. She swooped down, grabbed them, and darted away.

Ivan was nearly on me.

I flicked my wrist, turning my Fae bracelet into a dagger. "Don't even try it," I growled.

He was only a few feet from me, and his eerie eyes brightened as he looked at me, gleaming with triumph.

His gaze was right on my chest.

Orion's Heart.

I could feel it lying outside my shirt, the gem gleaming brightly. It had started pulsing in response to the power source, though that had stopped once I'd killed the spell.

Ivan began to chant the spell again, loud and clear.

He was on the last verse, though.

The paint on the ground began to glow again, the symbols going wild.

What the hell was he doing?

I charged, swiping out with my blade. He ducked and continued to chant.

Grey surged to his feet and charged Ivan.

The white-haired man reached for me, and I swiped out with my blade. It cut deeply into his forearm, but he was too quick. He grabbed Orion's Heart from my neck, breaking the chain.

He raised it upright as he chanted the last words of the spell. His face twisted with pain, and he released the gem. He'd held it for only a moment, but it was too late. His hand had turned black from the contact.

Overhead, the star-shaped window in the ceiling opened again. A beam of light rose from Orion's Heart and shot into the sky. The gem glowed as fiercely as the power source had. Even brighter.

"You carried this the entire time," Ivan's eyes gleamed with sadistic glee as he scrambled upright, looking toward the ceiling and the beam of light that grew stronger. "So much power in such a small stone. More than my power source. Enough to destroy all of Guild City."

The stone glowed between us, pulsing with a power that made my muscles tremble and my bones shake. Ivan gave me one last triumphant look, then ran for the door, sprinting through the fighting figures of our two small armies.

Horror yawned inside me as I watched the Orion's Heart pulse. The paint on the floor had begun to glow brightly as the magic transferred throughout the church.

How long did we have?

Grey neared me, his gaze going between me and the retreating Ivan. "Do you need help?"

"Go get him." I had no idea what I was going to do, only that I had to stop this. Deep in my gut, I knew I could stop it. And we couldn't let Ivan escape. He was capable of too much horror.

Grey charged past me in pursuit of Ivan.

Shaking, I stared at the pulsing gem, my mind racing. The spell had started again. I could feel it surging on the air, growing stronger with every minute. It would blow soon.

I could turn it back, but I had no container for it. Nothing to truly stop it. Without that, it would blow eventually.

It glowed brighter. Through the blinding light, it began to crack. A great roar sounded. The bomb was powering up. The magic would spin out of control and destroy us all.

We needed something, *anything*, to contain it.

I grabbed the stone and held it tightly in my palm.

Pain flared, agony like I'd never known.

I gripped it tightly, determined to force it back together. I had the briefest flash of knowledge—*this could kill me.*

Then the bomb exploded, blasting magic everywhere, a power so fierce that it felt like my skin was torn from my body and my bones were pulverized. I flew through the air and slammed to the ground.

Then power—such overwhelming power—expanded, and everything went dark.

17

Grey

Horrified, I watched Carrow crash to the ground, consumed in an aura of blinding light. For the briefest moment, she was a supernova. The power that pulsed through the church was enough to stop my heart for a second, and then it died.

The light faded, and Carrow lay still.

Terror shot through me.

At my feet, Ivan lay bound in the manacles I'd brought. The bastard had been so strong that I'd nearly been unable to get him.

I left him and sprinted for Carrow. My limbs felt like blocks of ice as I fell to my knees at her side. Her hands lay relaxed and open, and the ashes of Orion's Heart were scattered in her right palm.

The stone was gone.

Fear threatened to suffocate me as I gathered her close. She was pale as snow with dark shadows under her cheeks. The magic that pulsed from her was strong enough to burn me, making my skin vibrate where it touched hers.

But her life force...

I couldn't feel it.

"Carrow." My voice was rough. My heart thundered, a violent tattoo of fear inside my chest.

I couldn't lose her.

Not now.

Not *ever*.

I brushed her hair off her face. My blood could heal only physical injuries, and this could be magic.

But I had to try.

I bit into my wrist, tearing at the skin. Hastily, I raised my wrist to her slack mouth, pressing it to her lips.

She didn't move.

"Come on, Carrow. Wake up." Something inside me roared like a wounded animal.

Still, she didn't move.

Seconds passed.

She'd absorbed the power of the bomb. Instead of the spelling destroying us, it had taken her.

Mac fell to her knees at my side, a sob rising in her throat. Eve landed near us, stumbling. All around, the battle slowed. The only ones standing were from our side, so we must have won.

But I only had eyes for Carrow.

"Save her," Mac demanded.

"I'm trying, damn it."

Suddenly, Carrow shifted, her eyelids fluttering. Had my blood saved her, or was it her magic? It didn't matter. She was waking up.

Slowly, she blinked. "What happened?"

I hugged her to me, clutching her tight.

Mac jumped on us, hugging Carrow from behind. "You're all right!" Mac pulled back, confusion on her face. "You *are* okay, right?"

I released Carrow, lowering her so that I could look at her more closely.

She eased away from me, sitting upright under her own strength. Her eyes glowed with a strange light, nearly neon in their brightness.

"I...feel strange." She looked at her palms. The ashes of Orion's Heart marred her skin. "It's gone."

"You absorbed all the magic from Orion's Heart."

"It was going to explode," Carrow said, her voice slightly dazed. "It needed a vessel to contain it."

"So you decided to grab it," Mac said. "You're mad."

Carrow blinked. "I think I might be." Her gaze

darted around the room. "Where is Ivan? Did we get him?"

I nodded. "I've bound him. We'll take care of him." I was going to find a way to kill the bastard this time. "But how do you feel? Do we need to see a healer?"

"I honestly don't know." She rubbed her chest. "I feel different. More magical, maybe. I don't know."

Quinn arrived. He'd returned to human form, though he was covered with cuts and bruises. He looked at Carrow, his eyes intense. "We need to get out of here before the Council members escape their cell. We don't want them knowing what you just did."

"No one should know you're this powerful," Eve added.

They were right. It was a matter of safety now. Powerful supernaturals were feared, and in my long life, I'd never seen anyone do what Carrow had done. "Can you stand?"

"Not sure."

"I've got you." I stood, carefully picking her up and cradling her to my chest.

All around, the bodies of Ivan's men lay scattered. Mine were binding those still living and checking the bodies of the rest.

"I've got the main bastard," Quinn said, and looked toward one of my guards—Eloise. She was tall and strong, a black panther when she shifted. "Will you help me?"

She nodded. "Let's get him."

"Bring him to my place," I said.

Mac and Eve hurried alongside me as I carried Carrow from the church. She felt powerful in my arms, but weak still. Physically drained.

I hoped it was exhaustion and nothing more.

We stepped out into the fresh air. The blue dome had vanished. How the hell was I going to resist falling for her?

Carrow

Several days later, after I'd regained my strength, it was time to meet with the Council again. No one understood what had happened to me, but everyone vowed not to speak of it.

Grey had wanted me to stay at his place, but I'd insisted on going back to my own flat with Mac. My strength had finally returned, but I could feel the new magic going haywire inside me.

Now, I stood outside of Black Church with Mac. Guild City had returned to normal. The blue dome was gone, and Ivan had been taken care of. I hadn't asked Grey what he'd done with him. Something terrible, I had a feeling.

"You've got this," Mac said. "Your practice has paid off, and you're going to convince them you're in control."

"But I'm not," I murmured.

"That doesn't matter. What matters is what they think. Control your magical signature, and they won't know that your power is having a party inside you."

I chuckled, though it did nothing to lessen my nerves.

The door to Black Church opened, and Grey appeared, looking impossibly handsome in his impeccable suit. He'd arrived early to speak with some of the Council members.

Speak with.

That was the phrase he'd used. I had a feeling he planned to use mind manipulation and coercion, but since he'd be doing it on my behalf, I wasn't going to argue.

"They're ready for you." The concern in his eyes made me twitchy.

He'd had that same concern when he'd carried me from the church after I'd absorbed Orion's Heart.

He cared for me.

We hadn't talked about it—we'd hardly talked about anything since the bombing. All our time had been spent practicing my magic. And we didn't exactly have a relationship in which we talked about feelings.

I swallowed hard, uncertain of how to process it.

So I didn't.

Now wasn't the time, anyway. I didn't know if he cared for me, anyway, so no big deal.

"You've got this," Mac repeated, and squeezed my hand.

I squeezed hers back and walked toward Grey. "Let's get this over with."

"You'll have no trouble," he said, holding the door open for me.

He followed me inside, and we walked toward the main part of the church. The paint had been scrubbed from the floor and the place returned to normal, but I'd never forget the dark stain of Ivan's magic.

Walking toward the Council beside Grey was a big improvement from being dragged in wearing Magicuffs. Several of the Council members smiled at me. Most of them, in fact. They didn't know the exact role I'd played in saving us all, but they knew I'd been there and appreciated it. Even Ubhan didn't scowl quite as deeply as he had before, though he gave Grey a good, hard stare. The vampire and the sorcerers weren't *friendly*, but they were on better terms now that the sorcerers knew *why* we'd broken into their tower.

Ubhan stood. "You are here to demonstrate that you have control of your magic."

"Yes." I stopped in front of them, raising my arms. I drew in a steady breath and made sure I had my signature on tight lockdown, using the tricks that Grey had taught me. "As you can see, you can't sense it at all."

The Council members leaned forward, brows creased, as they tried to detect my magic. I stood perfectly still, keeping a tight rein on it by visualizing it as a monster trapped in a cage within my chest.

"Well, I'm impressed," Mateo said. "Not a hint of it."

"And I think we owe her a debt of thanks for her role in saving Guild City," said Cartimandua, the Witches' Guild leader.

"Of course." Ubhan nodded graciously. "We owe both of you our thanks."

The words were only slightly begrudging, and his eyes gleamed with sincerity. He'd been trapped in the cell while the whole thing had happened, able to feel the magic going out of control. He knew firsthand how close we'd all been to dying.

"You may approach the star now so that you can be assigned to your guild." Cartimandua smiled at me.

I stiffened, going a bit cold. "I didn't realize I'd be joining a guild now."

"Everyone joins a guild." Ubhan's voice hardened. "You've controlled your magic. Now the ceremony will know where to place you."

"Okay." I looked at Grey, who stood stiff and still.

"All will be well," he murmured.

I had the distinct feeling he didn't mean, *"No problem, you'll be chosen by a guild."* He meant, *"This will be fine, even if I have to kill them all."*

I gave him a weak smile and nodded, turning to walk

toward the metal star inlaid in the floor. Visions of Ivan flashed in my head, and I shook them away.

I needed to think witchy thoughts. That was the guild I'd choose, given a choice, though I wasn't keen on joining a guild at all.

When I reached the bronze star, I stopped, standing right beneath the window in the ceiling. Tension tightened my skin as I waited for the ceremony to begin.

Please don't knock me out.

I was getting damned sick of being knocked unconscious.

As one, the Council members leaned forward, watching me intently. I felt Grey's gaze on me, and I focused on his rather than the others'.

As it had the last time, a low chant began to echo around the room. It echoed, flowing through the space like water. Magic filled the air, pressing in on me. I looked up at a noise from above.

The star-shaped window in the ceiling was opening, and a shaft of light beamed down on me.

I braced myself, remembering the last time I'd stood in this light.

But this time, it glowed warmly on me. No pain.

I shifted, looking around the room. Was something supposed to happen?

The Council members looked at me, confusion flickering on their faces. Ubhan looked at the floor, then at me. "The magic isn't pointing to a guild."

"Yet she is not unconscious." Cartimandua's eyebrows rose. "You've grown stronger."

"Just had a good breakfast." I gave a weak smile.

"Uh-huh." She clearly didn't buy it for a second.

Grey stepped forward. "Something is clearly amiss with your ceremony. You should have that fixed."

Ubhan glowered. "That is not the case, and you know it."

"If the ceremony worked, she would be unconscious, or she would be assigned to a guild." Grey shrugged. "She is neither. Something has gone amiss. I expected better of the Council."

A low grumbling sounded from different corners of the room, but Cartimandua stood. "We don't know what is happening with the ceremony, but we can hardly return her to the prison."

"That is procedure!" Ubhan shouted.

"She helped save your hide, Ubhan." Cartimandua glowered at him. "Carrow must join a guild soon. If the ceremony doesn't work for her, we'll need to find another way to assign one. But in the meantime, we will vote on what to do with her."

I bristled. I didn't like the sound of this. The Council was *way* too involved in my life. But Cartimandua shot me a wink.

She had to know the vote would go in my favor, right? She'd been on my side all along. And I liked her.

I nodded. What choice did I have?

Cartimandua looked at each member of the Council. "Should Carrow stay free until she is assigned to a guild?" Her voice took on a heavier tone. "And do not forget the role she played in saving us all."

I waited, breath held, as the Council voted.

The no vote went first.

There were some real sticklers, it seemed, because four unfamiliar hands went up in support of keeping me in a holding cell until I was able to complete the ceremony. Ubhan's went up as well, making it five.

I felt sick to my stomach.

I could feel Grey at my side. The tension surrounding him was a physical thing. Were members of the Council allowed to abstain from voting? If so, and if there weren't enough votes in favor of letting me walk free, Grey would act.

And it wouldn't be pretty.

He hadn't so much as told me that he liked me—because *fond* certainly didn't count—and yet, I could feel that he would have my back.

When Cartimandua called for the vote to release me for the time being, the remaining Council members raised their hands.

Thank God.

Tension drained from my shoulders, but I stood straight. I didn't want them to know how worried I'd been.

"That is that." Cartimandua clapped her hands

together once. "You may go. But be warned, we will call you back soon to undergo the ceremony once more. In deference to the service you have done for Guild City, we will let this slide for now. But *only* for now."

"Thank you." I spun on my heel and left, getting the hell out of there as quickly as I could.

I didn't hear if Grey said anything to them, but his disapproval was apparent.

He joined me in the lobby, and we walked out. Silence fell heavily around us, and I remembered the sight of his terrified face as I woke up after the blast.

He'd been so worried for me.

I shot him a glance. How the hell we were going to go forward from here?

There was so much between us, none of it *normal.*

What were we?

We reached the main doors and stepped out into the sun.

Mac pounced. "Are you all right?"

"Fine."

"You passed?"

"I did."

"Do you have a guild?"

"No. And quit with the third degree. I'll explain later."

Mac glared at Grey. "Why didn't you fix it for her?"

It almost looked like he rolled his eyes, but the

Devil of Darkvale would never stoop to such a common thing. He ignored Mac and looked at me. "I'll see you soon."

"I'll—"

He turned and walked away.

Damn.

I shot Mac a look. "What a weirdo. Just walking away like that?"

She shrugged. "He's the Devil of Darkvale. He the *ultimate* weirdo." She sighed. "But he was really worried about you when we thought you were dead. You should have seen him."

I didn't know what to say, so I went with silence.

Mac grabbed my arm. "Come on. I've got something to show you."

She dragged me through the streets of Guild City. Since the dome had dropped, the mood of the city had been festive. The danger from Ivan hadn't lasted long, but it had been intense. The swell of dark magic that had rolled over the town had given its citizens a frightening glimpse of their possible fate, and when it had been averted, everyone wanted to celebrate.

A few minutes later, we reached our building. Mac shoved her way through the green door, which was already unlocked.

"Isn't that weird?" I asked. "It should be locked."

"Normally, yes." She raced up the stairs to my flat, flinging open the door.

I followed her. As soon as I peeked my head in, a chorus of voices shouted, "Surprise!"

I blinked.

My flat had been decorated, albeit in a haphazard fashion. Furniture of all different styles and colors filled the space, as well as crazy artwork on the walls featuring colorful animals.

Eve and Quinn stood inside. The witches I'd met last week, Beth, Coraline, and Mary, were also there, dressed in insane ensembles of feathers and colorful leather. It was a cool look. Cordelia sat on the couch, looking pleased as punch.

Balloons decorated the walls, and they all held glasses of champagne.

I grinned. "What is this?"

"Surprise party!" Eve said. "Your *official* welcome to town. We got you a few things for your place." She turned and gestured to a sign. "And also this."

The plaque was dark wood carved with scrolled white writing that read, CARROW BURTON: SUPERNATURAL SLEUTH.

Mac smiled. "We didn't know exactly what to call you, since your power is kind of weird. But you're good at solving mysteries, and I'd say that this last one was enough to prove you're ready to open your own shop."

"Wow." Tears pricked my eyes. "Thanks, guys." I walked to the sign and touched the edge. "This is way better than being a detective."

Quinn laughed. "Let's get you a glass of champagne."

I turned to my friends, happiness blooming inside me. My flat looked lovely, and though I still didn't know exactly where I was going to hang up my new shingle, I was excited to get started.

THANK YOU FOR READING!

I hope you enjoyed reading this book as much as I enjoyed writing it. Reviews are *so* helpful to authors. I really appreciate all reviews, both positive and negative. If you want to leave one, you can do so at Amazon or GoodReads.

ACKNOWLEDGMENTS

Thank you, Ben, for everything. There would be no books without you.

Thank you to Jena O'Connor, Lexi George, and Ash Fitzsimmons for your excellent editing. The book is immensely better because of you!

Thank you to Orina Kafe for the beautiful cover art.

AUTHOR'S NOTE

Hey there! I hope you enjoyed *Wicked Deal*. Most of the historical elements from this book were inspired by research trips to Romania and London. Some tidbits are too interesting not to share, but I don't want to bog down the book with them either, so I like to share them here in the author's note.

As I mentioned in the Author's Note for *Once Bitten*, Guild City and its guild towers were inspired by the town of Sighișoara in Transylvania, Vlad the Impaler's birthplace. It is an utterly beautiful, charming city that I wish I could have spent more time in.

There were many amazing parts of Sighișoara that did not make it into that book, including the Church on the Hill. The scene in *Wicked Deal* in which Carrow and Grey climb the narrow steps to the church to look for

Mariketta's crypt is based upon a church built in Sighișoara between 1429 and 1488.

In real life, it sits on a hill at the edge of Sighișoara, accessed by a set of stairs covered by a peaked wooden roof. They were build in 1642 to keep the snow off children as they climbed to a school near the church.

Inside the church, I invented the priest's office with the secret key. However, the crypt is based upon the one at the real church, which is accessed via a door inset into the floor near the front of the church. It is the only example of an ancient crypt in Transylvania, and it has been vandalized several times by thieves attempting to break into the crypts to find valuables. That damage is not easily seen now, however. The paintings on the interior walls of the church date to the 14th-16th centuries and are some of the rarest and most valued murals in Transylvania.

The restaurant owned by the Dwarves' Guild is based upon one that we visited in Brașov, a larger town about a three hours from Sighișoara. There were many underground restaurants and tunnels in Brașov, which were the inspiration for the ones in Guild City. Brașov was also the inspiration for the town that contained *La Papillon* and The Crescent Hotel.

As for the London Underground, the other inspiration for the Dwarves' territory, one must have a bit of a flexible imagination for how I laid that out. The bombed-out portions of the Tube that were destroyed in the Blitz are probably not so easily accessible today, but for the purposes of the story, the Dwarves have used magic to connect them to other parts of the Tube.

I borrowed two Victorian urban legends for the Underground. The first is that of Spring-Heeled Jack, a shadowy villain who lurked the streets of London. He first appeared in 1837, leaping out at a woman and tearing at her clothes with his claws. Later, he chased a carriage and leapt over a nine foot wall, hence the name. For roughly ten years, he was part of life in London, the product of superstition, mass hysteria, and newspaper stories that ignited the imaginations of Londoners.

The pigs of the Underground are another urban legend from the mid-19th century. During this time, the sewers were a relatively new invention in London. As such, they ignited the peoples' imaginations. According to the story, a sow managed to escape into the sewers, where she had a litter of pigs. The pig family survived off the scraps that were continually washed into the sewer, and it was said that one day they would escape and run rampant through the city.

Black Church in Guild City is based off of the real Black Church that sits in the center of Brașov. It is an impressively imposing structure with a blackened exterior. Construction began between 1383 and 1385 on the initially-Romance Catholic structure, but it wasn't completed until after 1476. During the Protestant reformation, the church was transitioned over to

Lutheran services. After invading Hapsburg forces set fire to the church in 1689, the exterior became blackened. Hence the name Black Church (*Biserica Neagră* in Romanian). For the story, I invented the entire interior, along with the dungeons that connect to the underground.

La Papillon, the posh bar that Carrow and Grey visited, was based on a secret bar accessed via a nearly hidden staircase in Brașov. Though that bar was far smaller than the one that I wrote, I loved the idea of a hidden speak-easy type bar for this book and so modified it to fit the story.

That's it for the history and myth in this book, though I will go into more detail about the very cool guild towers in future books. Thank you for reading, and I hope you stick around with Carrow and Grey for the rest of their adventures!

ABOUT LINSEY

Before becoming a writer, Linsey Hall was a nautical archaeologist who studied shipwrecks from Hawaii and the Yukon to the UK and the Mediterranean. She credits fantasy and historical romances with her love of history and her career as an archaeologist. After a decade of tromping around the globe in search of old bits of stuff that people left lying about, she settled down and started penning her own romance novels. Her Dragon's Gift series draws upon her love of history and the paranormal elements that she can't help but include.

COPYRIGHT

Published by Bonnie Doon Press LLC

Linsey@LinseyHall.com

www.LinseyHall.com

https://www.facebook.com/LinseyHallAuthor

Printed in Poland
by Amazon Fulfillment
Poland Sp. z o.o., Wrocław

58528852R00155